THE TEXAS TATTLER

All the news that's barely fit to print!

Fortunes Discover New Heirs

Scandal was the last thing Miranda Fortune wanted to bring her family when she returned to Red Rock with her son, Kane. But now it appears that the town won't be talking about the latest party this society matron has given—but the two infants she gave up for adoption!

According to Crazy Hearts Motel manager Hal Davies, an old rodeo cowboy pulled up to his establishment, looking for a room. "He was drunk as a skunk, but he claimed to be Kane and Gabrielle's daddy…and said he'd just tracked down their illegitimate siblings." P.I. Flynn Sinclair confirmed the rumor.

Local tongues are also wagging about Kane's *quick* engagement to nurse Allison Preston.

Sources at the hospital where both parties work said the couple had always acted more like friends than lovers. "But one day, we practically caught them doing the horizontal mambo in the staff lunchroom!" reports one surprised, unnamed staffer.

Don't know if there's any connection between these two events…but the *Tattler* can only wonder if any more shake-ups are in store for the powerful Fortune family!

Dear Reader,

Welcome to the world of Silhouette Desire, where you can indulge yourself every month with romances that can only be described as passionate, powerful and provocative!

Fabulous BJ James brings you June's MAN OF THE MONTH with *A Lady for Lincoln Cade*. In promising to take care of an ex-flame—and the widow of his estranged friend—Lincoln Cade discovers she has a child. Bestselling author Leanne Banks offers another title in her MILLION DOLLAR MEN miniseries with *The Millionaire's Secret Wish*. When a former childhood sweetheart gets amnesia, a wealthy executive sees his chance to woo her back.

Desire is thrilled to present another exciting miniseries about the scandalous Fortune family with FORTUNES OF TEXAS: THE LOST HEIRS. Anne Marie Winston launches the series with *A Most Desirable M.D.*, in which a doctor and nurse share a night of passion that leads to marriage! Dixie Browning offers a compelling story about a sophisticated businessman who falls in love with a plain, plump woman while stranded on a small island in *More to Love*. Cathleen Galitz's *Wyoming Cinderella* features a young woman whose life is transformed when she becomes nanny to the children of her brooding, rich neighbor. And Kathie DeNosky offers her hero a surprise when he discovers a one-night stand leads to pregnancy and true love in *His Baby Surprise*.

Indulge yourself with all six Desire titles—and see details inside about our exciting new contest, "Silhouette Makes You a Star."

Enjoy!

Joan Marlow Golan

Joan Marlow Golan
Senior Editor, Silhouette Desire

Please address questions and book requests to:
Silhouette Reader Service
U.S.: 3010 Walden Ave., P.O. Box 1325, Buffalo, NY 14269
Canadian: P.O. Box 609, Fort Erie, Ont. L2A 5X3

A Most Desirable M.D.

ANNE MARIE WINSTON

Silhouette

Desire

Published by Silhouette Books

America's Publisher of Contemporary Romance

Special thanks and acknowledgment are given to Anne Marie Winston for her contribution to The Fortunes of Texas: The Lost Heirs series.

 SILHOUETTE BOOKS

ISBN 0-373-76371-9

A MOST DESIRABLE M.D.

Visit Silhouette at www.eHarlequin.com

Printed in U.S.A.

Books by Anne Marie Winston

Silhouette Desire

Best Kept Secrets #742
Island Baby #770
Chance at a Lifetime #809
Unlikely Eden #827
Carolina on My Mind #845
Substitute Wife #863
Find Her, Keep Her #887
Rancher's Wife #936
Rancher's Baby #1031
Seducing the Proper Miss Miller #1155
*The Baby Consultant #1191
*Dedicated to Deirdre #1197
*The Bride Means Business #1204
Lovers' Reunion #1226
The Pregnant Princess #1268
Seduction, Cowboy Style #1287
Rancher's Proposition #1322
Tall, Dark & Western #1339
A Most Desirable M.D. #1371

*Butler County Brides

ANNE MARIE WINSTON

Pennsylvania native Anne Marie Winston loves babies she can give back when they cry, animals in all shapes and just about anything that blooms. When she's not writing, she's chauffeuring children to various activities, trying *not* to eat chocolate or reading anything she can find. She will dance at the slightest provocation, occasionally gets suckered into amateur theater performances and weeds her gardens when she can't see the sun for the weeds anymore. You can learn more about Anne Marie on the Harlequin/Silhouette Web site at www.eHarlequin.com.

THE FORTUNES OF TEXAS™

Meet the Fortunes of Texas

Meet the Fortunes of Texas's Lost Heirs. Membership in this Texas family has its privileges and its price. As the family gathers to welcome their newest members, they discover a murderer in their midst...and passionate new romances that only a true-bred Texas love can bring!

CAST OF CHARACTERS

Dr. Kane Fortune: While Kane's verdict was still out on his new relatives, this doctor knew that no Fortune walked away from his responsibilities. And he was an honorable man.

Allison Preston: Fate had just made plain-Jane Allison Preston's secret wish come true. But her dream was about to become a nightmare unless she could make Kane Fortune see that he belonged with her forever....

Miranda Fortune: This Fortune heiress had been estranged from her family for over twenty-five years, but now the secret that drove her out of Red Rock, Texas, is about to be revealed!

One

Dr. Kane Fortune slammed through the doors of County General Hospital in San Antonio, Texas, frustration and fury eating at his gut like a living thing. Damn, but he hated to lose a patient. Hated it, hated it, *hated* it.

He supposed every doctor did, but somehow the babies always seemed the worst to him. This one had been particularly tough. The young father had broken down and cried until they'd had to call his family physician in to offer comfort and medication. That guy had wanted his child so much…too bad every father in the world didn't care that deeply. The anger that bubbled up from far down inside him was old and bitter. If *he* ever had children, he'd be there for them every step of the way. He took a sharp left across the parking lot, striding toward the rugged Ford Explorer he'd bought while he still lived in California, his head down, hands jammed in his trouser pockets.

He almost ran the woman down before he realized she was standing in his path.

"Whoa—I'm sorry." He reached out automatically to steady her, cupping her elbow, and only then did he realize who it was.

"Allison." He stopped, still holding her elbow, thunderstruck.

Allison Preston was a pediatric nurse with whom he worked on a near-daily basis in the neonatal unit. She was steady, sensible, reliable, and without question his favorite person in the hospital. They'd gotten into the habit of having coffee together once or twice a week if they happened to be in the cafeteria or the staff lounge at the same time. He still wasn't sure how it had happened, but Allison had become the one person in whom he could confide the pressures of the life-altering decisions he was often forced to make. He'd actually begun to anticipate when she would take her breaks and time himself so that his would coincide. She was the best listener he'd ever met, and her quiet understanding had soothed him on more than one occasion.

But the Allison standing before him wasn't the pale, buttoned-down nurse with her blond hair scraped back in a severe bun to whom he was accustomed. This Allison had yards and yards of thick, bouncy, curling sunlit tresses that she'd been in the process of unpinning when he'd nearly run her down. The curls cascaded around her shoulders and down her back, glowing in the early morning light with an almost unnatural sheen as they slithered free of the bun. The jolt he'd given her had sent one wayward lock flying across her face and he watched, mesmerized, as she hooked a finger through the curl and tugged it aside.

"Dr. Fortune. Kane," she said belatedly, when he pointed a finger at her, silently reminding her that he'd told her to call him Kane when they weren't working. "I'm sorry, too. I should have been paying more attention."

"I, uh, I was distracted." The words were a lame effort. He still couldn't believe it was the same woman he thought he knew. "I've never seen you with your hair down," he said slowly. "You have…a lot of hair."

A faint hint of pink color crept into her cheeks and she ducked her head in a self-conscious manner he recognized. "A mess, you mean," she corrected. "I've thought about getting it cut, but I just haven't gotten around to it."

He didn't say anything. He wanted to beg her not to cut it, to tell her that hair like that was every man's fantasy, that he could imagine wrapping himself in that gorgeous mane, could see it streaming around him while—

What the hell was he thinking? This was *Allison,* for God's sake. His co-worker. His friend, if he could call her that. His confidante.

"Kane?" She was eyeing him curiously, the emerald eyes that were one of her most striking features wide with concern. "Are you okay?" She put her hand on his arm and patted gently, comfortingly. "The Simonds' baby didn't make it, did she?"

Her hand was warm on his arm, drawing him back to the present and he shook his head silently as the reasons for his lack of concentration returned.

"You did everything you could, you know." She continued touching his arm now, a light, soothing stroke. "I knew if she survived the week it would be a miracle." She sighed. "And let's face it, with the number of premature infants we see with serious problems, miracles don't come along often enough."

"It still tears me apart," he admitted quietly, the regret he still felt at losing the baby welling within him again.

She tilted her head and smiled sympathetically at him.

"That's not a bad thing, you know. It's one of the reasons you're the best doctor on this staff. You care."

He shook his head. "Too much, sometimes." He lifted a hand and scrubbed it over his face, massaging his temple. "I'm whipped. I was up almost all night with that case, and I've got rounds in a few hours. I'm going to try to grab some sleep."

She nodded. "My shift just ended at seven. I'm headed home, too." She stepped back, hesitated, then lifted her hand again and briefly squeezed his shoulder. "Get some rest. And try not to feel so badly. She was lucky to have had you for a doctor."

And with one last smile, she climbed into a little red Mazda and backed out of the parking space, giving him a long study of her classical profile before she drove away.

Kane stood there, watching until she was out of sight. A red sports car. If he'd ever considered what kind of car she drove, he'd have guessed a sensible compact or a small sedan in a dark color that wouldn't attract a lot of notice. It was a shock, although he didn't quite know why. Just like the hair. Maybe Allison wasn't as sensible and passionless as the image she projected.

When he realized he was massaging the shoulder she'd touched, he dropped his hand and grimaced. God, he must be tired. He'd never been an indiscriminate skirt-chaser and he didn't usually get the hots for quiet little nurses, but here he stood, wondering what Allison Preston would look like lying beneath him with all that glorious hair spread across the pillow.

Probably damned good. He was a male, after all. He'd noticed the trim little butt beneath her uniform pants and he'd eyed her breasts from time to time, wondering if they looked so full because her waist was so small or her uniform top was loose...or because they *were* full and round and delicious. But he'd always stopped himself from finding out with the reminder that a good friend was a hard commodity to come by. Allison was one of the few women he knew who didn't seem to want anything from him. Most women, even if they didn't know about his family connections, wanted either sex or marriage or both. The rest simply added money and prestige to that list.

But Allison wasn't like the women who sought him out on a near-daily basis, and he found his interest level rising. She was gentle and soft and if he were honest, he'd admit that he'd wondered if she'd be that gentle and soft in bed, or if he could get her to turn into a demanding wildcat beneath his hands.

Stop it, he told himself. *Allison would be mortified if she knew what you were thinking.*

Banishing the images teasing his mind, he walked on across the lot to his car and drove out to his mother's villa in Kingston Estates, not far from the hospital. It was one of the newest communities in San Antonio, an enclave of indecent wealth, and his mother's home was no exception. The sight of her sprawling Mediterranean-style villa always took him aback for an instant no matter how many times he came by.

He'd grown up in modest circumstances—modest, ha! That was an understatement. His mother had barely been able to keep a roof over her children's heads for most of his life. He'd worked his butt off in school to keep his grades high, knowing that his only chance at med school was on scholarships and loans. Then, six years ago, his sister had discovered that their mother hadn't been entirely truthful with her children.

He and Gabrielle always had assumed she had no family…which was laughable now that they knew the truth. Miranda had family in spades, though she'd been estranged from them after a fight with her father years before Kane's birth.

Although Kane's mother had resisted the idea of reconciliation at first, his sister Gabrielle had badgered her until finally Miranda had softened. The father with whom she'd always clashed had passed away, and Miranda's brother Ryan had welcomed her back into the family fold—the family that had turned out to be one of the wealthiest clans in Texas, the Fortunes.

When his mother had decided to reclaim the Fortune name, everything had changed. They'd gone from being a threesome to being part of a…a tribe. True, the tribe had been uniformly warm and welcoming, but it was still overwhelming to have a hundred relatives instead of two.

To Kane's shock and surprise, that welcome had included sharing his grandfather's extremely large estate with Miranda. His mother, a woman who had elevated scrimping and saving to an art form, now was one of the most well-to-do heiresses in the country.

Kane still wasn't sure how he felt about the Fortune money. He didn't begrudge his mother her welcome back to the life into which she'd been born. She deserved to take it easy after all the rough years.

One thing he was sure of, though—he didn't want it. He'd gotten used to forging his own path and he didn't intend to let anyone tell him what to do. Accepting money, even family money that his mother insisted was due him, felt too much like charity. He was used to working for what he wanted and he preferred to keep it that way. And there was another reason he shied away from his inheritance, his heritage. That money was an obligation. It didn't come free, but with many, many strings to the people who made up his mother's family. He'd learned early that people who gave you something usually wanted something in return, and he suspected the Fortunes were no different, though none of them had proven his theory. Yet.

So far the only thing he'd allowed the Fortunes to give him was their name. And that was only because he liked bearing the name of the slimeball who'd abandoned his mother even less.

As he pulled the Explorer to a halt in the circular drive fronting the red-roofed stucco house, the deep melancholy that had plagued him returned. He dragged himself from the car and used the house key his mother had given him for situations just like this, letting himself into the cool house and heading for the kitchen.

"Kane!" As he passed the dining room, his mother glanced up and saw him, and her blue eyes crinkled into a warm smile as she rose. "I wasn't expecting you."

He stopped in the doorway. "I wasn't expecting me, either. But I only have a few hours until rounds, and home was too far away."

Even this early in the morning, with no makeup and her blond hair caught back in a loose, low knot, Miranda Fortune was still a beautiful woman. Though she'd worked like a dog during his childhood to eke out a decent life for him and Gabrielle, she'd retained the striking good looks possessed by so many of the Fortune clan.

His clan. His family. The same characteristics that looked at him in the mirror every morning. Or evening. Or whenever the hell he had time to shave.

The thought reminded him of how wiped out he was. "Do you mind if I crash here for a while?"

"Of course not." She came toward him, stretching up to kiss him on the cheek. "Go. Find a bed. You look exhausted."

He did, stopping only to snag a plateful of leftover chicken and cucumber salad from the cook, which he inhaled standing up while the small Mexican woman chattered a stream of Spanish at him warning him of the dire consequences of gobbling his meal. Five minutes later, he was pulling off his boots and sinking into the firm king mattress in the bedroom he customarily took when he visited his mother.

He was in a deep, dreamless sleep when the ringing of the telephone near his bed jerked him from slumber. Startled, too sleepy to be coherent, he shot out a hand and grabbed the receiver, holding it to his ear to marshal his thoughts before speaking. It was probably a page from the hospital.

But before he could speak, the sound of a man's voice caught his attention.

"...thought you'd be glad to hear from me, honey. After all, I am the father of your children. Some of 'em, at least."

"It's only eight-thirty in the morning. What do you want?" His mother's voice was thin and quavering, totally unlike her normal tones.

"Figured I'd catch you before you started your daily socialite routine." There was a wheedling note in the man's tone. "I only want a little teeny-tiny somethin' that you have enough of not to miss."

"Money." Miranda's tone was stronger, flat with disgust. "I should have known it would take money to bring you out of the woodwork, Lloyd."

Lloyd...! It was his father. Lloyd Wayne Carter. The man whose surname he'd had the misfortune to bear most of his life even though the man himself had taken off without a backward glance before his second child was even born.

"I got a letter from our little daughter Gabrielle, y'know. Looked me up and wanted to let me know I was a granddaddy. Surprised the heck out of me to find out that my little Randi's rollin' in money, I can tell you. How come you never shared any of that money with me when we were married?''

''That's not your business.'' Miranda tried to inject assurance into her tone. ''You took yourself out of my life almost thirty years ago. I don't want you back in it now.''

''Well, that's a real shame, 'cause our little girl wants me. Invited me to come and visit, see my grandbaby. Wasn't that sweet?'' Carter spoke in a sugary tone that made Kane grit his teeth. Then a sound in the background caught his attention. It sounded like a woman, furiously whispering. But he couldn't make out the words.

''Don't you dare come here! You stay away from me and my children! You didn't have a thing to do with raising them, you—you—''

''Now, Randi, calm down—''

''I will *not* calm down—''

''Or this conversation ends and I go straight to—''

''No. No! Please don't tell him.''

''Then ante up, sweetheart. He lives right there in San Antonio, y' know.'' Kane definitely heard a woman's voice this time, but the sound was drowned out as his mother sucked in an anguished breath.

''I've kept your little secret for a long time, and I deserve something for it, don't you think?''

''How much?'' Kane had never heard his mother's voice sound so dull and lifeless. ''How much do you want, Lloyd, to get out of my family's life again for good?''

''Hmm. I'm not a greedy man, Randi honey. How about twenty-five thousand for each twin? That should get me out of my present unfortunate circumstances and leave me a little to get by on.''

''*Fifty thousand?*'' Miranda sounded genuinely stunned. ''You can't be serious!''

''As a heart attack, honey.'' Carter guffawed at his own

wit. "With all the money you got when you rejoined your loving family after ol' Kingston kicked off, you'll never even miss it."

"Don't you speak my father's name, you pig." Miranda's voice was shaking. "My father was—"

"I guess this is a little bit of a shock," Carter broke in. "Tell ya what. I'll give you some time to think it over. I'll be coming to San Antonio to see my little daughter and granddaughter, maybe look up my fine son in a few weeks. I'll see you then, honey, and we can square this deal."

"You don't have a deal." But there was no force behind Miranda's words.

"Oh, I'll have a deal," he promised. "Or I'll be lookin' up a certain oil man and askin' him how his twins are."

Miranda made an incoherent sound.

"See ya soon, Randi. We'll have ourselves a real fine family reunion." And he ended the connection.

"Oh my God. Oh my God. Oh my God."

Kane realized his mother hadn't replaced the receiver. He took the stairs to the first floor two at a time, his chest heaving and his hands shaking with tension. Bursting into the dining room where his mother still sat, the phone in one hand and a shocked, blank expression on her face, he demanded, "I was listening in. What the hell did that bastard want? What did he mean about 'the twins'?"

"Don't curse, dear," his mother said. Then her breath hitched, and to his horror, she burst into tears.

Allison Preston entered the staff lounge at seven-thirty that evening and went straight to her locker. Thank God her four-day week ended after tomorrow's day shift. Twelve-hour shifts were bad enough, but she'd no sooner gotten home in the morning than she'd gotten a frantic call from her supervisor. One of the other nurses had come down with the flu.

Since Allison lived close to the hospital she was often the first one called in a crisis. And she usually didn't mind. After all, it wasn't as if her life was so busy she couldn't rearrange her social calendar.

So, when the phone call came, she'd turned right around and come back to the hospital and worked another twelve-hour shift. Twenty-fours always played havoc with her system. She just wanted to go home and fall into bed.

Then she realized she wasn't alone in the room. Kane Fortune sat in a chair with his large, competent hands dangling between his knees. He appeared to be staring into space and his handsome features were drawn and wan. She wasn't even sure he knew she was there.

Quietly, she approached him and sat down next to him. "Are you all right?"

He blinked, and she could almost see him dragging himself back to the present. He seemed to weigh his words for a moment, and then he shrugged. "Frankly, no."

"Still brooding about the Simonds' baby?"

"It's more than that," he said.

"Oh? Do you want to talk about it?"

Kane turned his head and looked at her, and the punch of hot desire she felt every time he turned those green-hazel eyes on her hit her hard in the stomach and quickly sank to a much more intimate location. Sweet heavens, he was beautiful. And she'd swear he didn't know it.

Or if he did, he didn't particularly care.

The first time she'd ever seen him had been four years ago, on her very first day on the job at County. He'd come into the neonatal unit for rounds, and the supervisor had introduced them. He'd turned those eyes on her and smiled and taken her hand—and she'd been lucky to be able to stammer out a garbled greeting.

That was just how strongly he affected her. Always had. And, she thought ruefully, always would. For the first year she'd told herself it was just a crush. Young, inexperienced-in-more-ways-than-one nurse; handsome, wealthy doctor. Normal. Natural. By the end of the second year, when she realized she still loved him no matter how tired he looked or how cranky he got with incompetent staff members, she started to worry about herself. By the end of the third year, when she realized he could be penniless and jobless and she'd still care, she'd accepted it.

Kane Fortune was the only man she ever wanted to own her heart. And the chances of that were about as likely as her chances of...of winning an Oscar.

Not going to happen. Not now, not ever. Men like Kane didn't go for mousy blondes who weren't comfortable in deep-cut blouses and makeup. They went for glamor. Just as her father had. And there was no way anyone could ever accuse plain little Allison Jane Preston of being glamorous. Plain Allison Jane.

"It would take half the night," he said. "More time than you have, I'm sure."

For a moment she thought he'd been reading her mind and was making a dig at the thought of her getting gussied up. Then she realized he meant time to talk. Tired as she was, all thoughts of bed and sleep went straight out the window. It sounded as though Kane needed a friend, and she didn't intend to let him down.

"I'm off for the next twelve hours, and I'm a good listener," she said. Not pushing, but letting him know she was there if he needed her.

He was smiling faintly at her, one hand coming up to scrub at the dark shadow of stubble along his jaw. "Yes, you are." Then he appeared to come to a decision. "Want to go get a bite to eat?"

"Sure." She tried to keep the giddy elation from her voice. They'd gotten coffee and chatted dozens of times over the past few years. Kane had seemed to single her out as someone with whom he felt comfortable, and loving him as she did, Allison was always grateful when she could give him a listening ear, ease the burdens that came with healing newborn bodies and occasionally losing the battle for life. But dinner after work, not on a hasty break in the hospital when one or the other of them was wolfing down a quick bite...this was different.

"Let's go down to the diner," he said.

"All right." The diner was an all-night restaurant near County that was frequented by hospital personnel and the occasional repeat visitor who had gotten wise to hospital cafeteria food.

She stood and started to shoulder the large bag in which she carried extra clothes, but Kane reached for it, taking it from her and slinging it over his shoulder with his own duffel. "Thank you," she said, mildly startled. How many men were that courteous anymore?

"My pleasure." He smiled down at her as he opened the door for her, and her legs turned to jelly. "My mama raised a gentleman."

"Your mama did a fine job."

"She did," he said reflectively as they waited for the elevator. "She was a single mother, but she worked darn hard to make sure my sister and I grew up with good manners and good sense."

"Your father...wasn't in the picture?" It was a personal question, the first time they'd ever crossed the line into such territory, and she wondered if he was as aware of that as she.

"No. Never." There was such venom in his tone that it unnerved her. "He abandoned us when my mother was pregnant with my sister. I was about a year old."

"That's sad," she said softly. "He missed so much. It's a good thing your mother had money, or things could have been really tough for you all."

A smile touched his lean face as she glanced up at him, but it wasn't amused. "We didn't have money then," he said. "I didn't even find out she was a Fortune until about six years ago."

Now she was confused. "But your name—"

"I took the name Fortune by choice, and at my uncle's request, not long after I found out. I had no desire to share the name of a man who could walk away from his family the way he did."

She wondered if he realized how much unhappiness was revealed in that simple statement. "My father left my mother, too," she said softly, wanting him to know she could identify in some way with his pain. "But I remember him. I was twelve when he left."

"At least you knew your father."

"Yes." Though she wasn't sure that knowing him had made any difference, since she apparently *hadn't* known him at all. A too-familiar pain and regret stung her. He was dead now and she'd never have the chance to talk with him again, and the estrangement that had lain between them for years could never be bridged. She'd missed the opportunity, or more accurately, she'd *refused* the opportunity. And now, to her lasting regret, it was too late.

Still, she didn't tell any of that to Kane. In the mood he was in, she doubted there was anything she could say that might ease his hurt. For a while they walked along the sidewalk in silence.

When they got to the diner, Kane paused, and Allison

stopped with him. He was looking through the plate-glass window. "There's a crowd tonight," he said, frowning.

"Birthday party," she said. "One of the techs from radiology turned forty."

A slim, dark-haired nurse from the oncology unit caught sight of them from the edge of the dance floor where there were a number of people gyrating to the music. She waved, her gaze on Kane, a slow smile lighting her big dark eyes as her hips swiveled in time to the beat. She beckoned for them to enter, but Allison was aware of Kane shaking his head.

She looked in at the rowdy, raucous crowd, whose jovial spirit could clearly be heard on the street. The girl was vivacious, confident in her own sex appeal—exactly the kind of woman she'd expect Kane to be attracted to—and her heart contracted. But when she glanced up at him, Kane seemed reluctant to enter despite the blatant invitation the girl was giving him.

She was fiercely glad that he didn't seem in the mood for a party. She didn't want to share him with anyone. "If you're not thrilled about the crowd," she said slowly, wondering if she was crazy even to be making the offer, "we can go to my house. It's not far. We could stop and get some Chinese takeout."

Kane's eyes were still on the crowd inside.

"But maybe that's not something that interests you," she said hastily, feeling the heat of embarrassment coloring her cheeks. Of course Kane Fortune wasn't interested in spending a quiet evening alone with plain Allison Jane.

Then Kane turned to her, and there was warm approval in his eyes. "It sounds great," he said, and there was genuine pleasure in his tone. "And I appreciate the offer very much. How about I follow you in my car?"

* * *

She still couldn't believe he was *here*. Kane Fortune. Sitting on her sofa beside her, empty cartons from the Chinese food on the small glass table in her dining area mute proof that he really had been here and eaten a meal with her. Right now he was toying with the end of a lock of her hair, which he'd teased her into taking down the minute they'd gotten into her house. "I like it down," he'd said. And that had been enough for her.

He picked up the wine bottle they were sharing, indicating her glass, but she put a cautious hand over the rim of her glass. "Better not. I don't do alcohol real well."

He grinned, a pirate's rakish smile. "Oh, good. Here, have some more."

She laughed, tucking one foot beneath her and angling her body to face him more fully. "I think not." It was an incredible, heady feeling, teasing and flirting with him. But it was time to help him now. She hadn't forgotten the initial reason for this whole visit. It wasn't as if it were a date, after all. "At the risk of wrecking the mood, I'd really like to hear what's bothering you, if you'd still like to talk it out."

He sobered immediately, the gold glints in his eyes dimming and his smile fading. "I don't think I'd better get started. It's a long and ugly story, as I said."

"I'm a good listener, remember? And a good friend. And that's what friends are for, to share burdens." She put her hand on his arm, right on his bare skin, and rubbed her thumb lightly over the hair-roughened, sinewy flesh.

Kane put his hand over hers, squeezing lightly. "You're a treasure, Allison. I value our friendship."

The words were a balm to her hungry heart, the sweetest sounds she'd ever heard and the last ones she'd ever have expected. She hadn't expected *anything*. She could never hope to have Kane's love, but she was grateful at least to hold his friendship.

He sighed, removing his hand from atop hers and dropping his head back against the cushions of her sofa, slouching so his long body stretched bonelessly and his hip grazed the knee she'd drawn up beneath her. "You asked me about the Simonds' baby this morning. And you were right. I was upset. Angry, too. I've spent years in school learning how to save pre-term infants, and it really gets to me when I fail." He tried to smile, but the effort died before it really got going. "I guess I want to be God."

She didn't comment, but she kept her hand on his arm, lightly stroking as she sensed the tension within him.

"Anyway," he went on, "I decided to sleep at my mother's for the few hours before rounds, since her home is much closer to the hospital than mine. But I was awakened by a phone call." His voice grew taut and angry and he stopped abruptly.

"Someone who made you mad," she ventured.

"Someone who made me *furious,*" he corrected. "Only he didn't know I was on the phone. He was talking to my mother." His lips thinned and his nostrils flared in disgust. "It was my father. All of a sudden this creep who's been gone for three decades just can't wait to see us again."

"But…why?"

"My sister." He rolled his head toward Allison and their eyes met. His softened fondly and his tone was wry. "Gabrielle's always been a soft touch. She has a little girl of her own now and she recently thought it only decent to let dear old Dad know. I have no idea how she found him but she invited him to come down here and visit." His tone grew hard again. "I'd strangle her barehanded if I thought she had any idea what she started. But I know she was just following her heart."

"So, your father's coming to San Antonio?" She could see why he would be upset, but the fury that seemed to be so tightly coiled beneath the surface was almost too much. It wasn't like Kane to overreact. And she should know, since she'd worked with him in situations where grieving people did all kinds of bizarre things, occasionally aimed at the hapless physician whose skill hadn't been enough to save their loved one.

"Yeah, but that's not the worst of it." Kane sprang to his feet so quickly she jumped back, startled, and he began to pace the length of her small living area like a great tiger confined within a small cage. "He threatened my mother. *Blackmailed* her, actually."

"Blackmailed?" It was so weird she just blurted it out. "What kind of secret could your mother have that would invite blackmail?"

He wheeled and looked across the room at her, and his eyes were wild. "My mother," he said slowly, enunciating each syllable, "ran away from home when she was seventeen. She told us she just couldn't get along with her father, but it turns out she was pregnant. She was headed for California but she got hung up in Nevada where she had her babies—twins, a boy and a girl—and gave them up for adoption. Actually," he said, "she left them on the steps of the sheriff's office with notes pinned to their blankets."

"Your poor mother." Allison's heart was soft; she could imagine the young, pregnant woman's desperation.

"Yeah. She was young, not even twenty, and I suppose she was about at rock bottom financially and too proud to go home—"

"And her self-esteem was probably rock bottom as well," she interjected softly.

"Probably," he agreed. "Soon afterward, she met *my*

father. Lloyd Carter was a rodeo cowboy. They got married and I was born nine months later. By the time I was a year old, she was pregnant again. Very shortly after he found out, my prize of a father took off for greener pastures.''

The thought of a young woman, barely twenty years old and pregnant for the third time, probably grieving over her lost children and her poor choices, brought tears to Allison's eyes. Instinctively, she reached out a hand to Kane, and he took it briefly, dropping back onto the couch beside her with his head in his hands.

''Carter's threatened to tell the biological father about the twins,'' he said. ''If my mother doesn't pay him fifty thousand.''

She sucked in a sharp, horrified breath. ''Where in the world—'' Then she remembered to whom she was speaking. ''She has the money?''

Kane nodded. ''But neither of us thinks that'll be the end of the matter.'' His voice shook with contained rage and he slammed one fist into the other. ''I *hate* not being able to fix this! All my life I've tried to help, to make things easier for my mother.'' His tone lowered and filled with such hopelessness that it tore at Allison's heart. ''And this time there's not a thing I can do.''

''Oh, Kane, just being there for your mother is doing something.'' Allison looped her arms around his shoulders and leaned her forehead against him, hugging him tightly. If only there was something she could do to relieve the anguish he was living!

''I can't explain to you how strange it feels to know I have a brother and a sister out there somewhere whom I've never met. We'll never share childhood memories,'' he said slowly. ''For my mother, it's like it all happened yesterday. I had to sedate her. God, it was hellish.''

Allison urged him to her, cradling him and rocking instinctively as he reached for her, burying his head in her neck and clutching her so tightly she could barely breathe. For the longest time, she simply held him, loving the whisper of his warm breath over her neck and the hard clasp of his arms around her. If this was the closest she would ever get to Heaven, she was going to memorize every second of it to relive later when the real world and loneliness returned.

Kane moved then, and she started to withdraw her arms from around him, aware that this was probably more comfort than he'd needed or wanted. But before she could move away, he turned to her, lifting one large hand to cradle her cheek. "Thank you," he whispered. "For listening."

"You're welcome." But her voice died away to nothing. He was looking at her lips. She held herself perfectly, utterly still as he smoothed his thumb along her bottom lip, and then, as his head came down, she realized that Kane was going to kiss her.

Two

Allison was pliant and as still as a frightened doe beside him. Her mouth trembled beneath his, her lips stayed chastely closed. Kane wanted to devour every inch of her delectable body, and he had to force himself not to give in to the wild surge of unbridled lust that urged him to grab her and drag her down beneath him.

He knew this was wrong, that he was taking advantage of her friendship, and he knew he'd be sorry forever if he drove her away. But he couldn't have stopped himself from kissing her if the world was ending. She was warm and sweet and soft and he needed her warmth to fill the cold ache inside him, needed her sweetness to counter the bitter surge of anger, needed her soft body to sheathe him and give him succor. He slid his tongue along the seam of her lips, using a little pressure, and to his delight, she slowly opened her mouth to admit him.

She was hesitant and shy, her tongue gently touching his

at first, and it struck him that she'd never denied him anything. He still wasn't sure what had possessed him to spill his family closet's skeletons tonight, but it had felt so *right* to confide his fears and worries and furies, to give all those emotions into her care and let her wrap him in her own unique brand of comfort, that he didn't question the impulse. Just as he didn't question the direction in which he was moving now. It felt right. *She* felt right.

"Allison," he muttered. "I need you." He slid both arms around her and pulled her into his embrace, never ceasing his gentle tactical assault on her mouth. *Please, please,* his body begged, and he shivered with pleasure when her arms came around him more fully and her fingers speared into his hair, pressing his mouth harder on hers. He unleashed a bit more of the hungry beast prowling inside him then, thoroughly exploring her mouth with his tongue, dipping and licking and plunging repeatedly into her sweetness.

Her breath was coming faster; she twisted in his arms. He pressed her backward against the couch until she lay prone against the cushions and he lay half over her. Her body was lush and giving and he rubbed restlessly against her thigh as one hand came around to her blouse and tugged it free of her pants, slipping his palm over silky belly and the slight ridges of ribs until he reached the lower swell of a breast. He halted momentarily, afraid to startle her by moving too suddenly. But she didn't appear to be skittish, and he slipped his fingers beneath the edge of her bra. Slowly, he filled his palm with soft, heavy woman flesh, almost groaning aloud as her tender nipple became a taut little nub beneath his stroking hand.

Carefully he eased his other hand from beneath her, all of his senses centered on the ultimate prize now. He unbuttoned his shirt one-handed and shrugged it back off his shoulders. When her small hands stroked over his bared flesh and explored his chest, he did groan beneath his breath, encouraging her without breaking the moment with words. Words were beyond him anyway; all he could do was *feel*. Her hands grew busier, yanking at his shirt until it was tossed aside on the floor.

And then it was his turn. He opened her shirt with the same dexterous touch he'd used on his own, still kissing and petting her, until he could shove the fabric away from her torso. She arched up, allowing him access to the clasp of her bra, and he thanked God for an old high school trick he'd perfected, of flicking open a bra fastening with one hand. The bra loosened. He tugged her toward him so she could shrug out of both garments and when she did, he drew away from her mouth for the first time, his hungry gaze devouring the bounty before him.

"You are so beautiful," he whispered hoarsely. He'd been right about her breasts, and yet he'd been wrong. His imagination couldn't begin to compare to the ripe, soft flesh that greeted him. He looked up from the full, perfect globes of her breasts tipped in the palest of pink crests, into her eyes, smiling at the look of stunned, hope-filled pleasure he saw there. "So beautiful," he repeated. And then he lowered his head and took one of those tempting tips into his mouth. He suckled gently at first. She sucked in a sharp breath and cried out, and then her hand came up to hold his head to her as he increased the pull on her tender flesh, drawing her deep into his mouth and swirling his tongue around her. The gesture of acceptance inflamed him beyond restraint and finally he had to have more. He quickly unfastened her pants, opening them and shoving both her slacks and panties down and off in one motion.

For the first time, she appeared to withdraw a little, shrinking into herself the tiniest bit. Some men might not have noticed, might not have cared, but he wanted, *needed* Allison to be his in every way there was, to give him every ounce of her generous warmth and the passion he sensed unfurling within her. He spread one big hand on her belly, gentling her, raising his head and returning to persuade her with his lips on hers. His hand gradually inched down the soft plane of her abdomen until he was brushing the soft cloud of curls at her thighs.

His whole body tensed at the tantalizing touch. He wanted to slide down her slim length, to place his mouth on every inch of her fragrant, scented sweetness, but he knew she wasn't ready for that. Instead, he simply extended one finger along the plump folds of flesh that protected her feminine secrets, gently increasing the pressure until her body gave way and admitted him to a hot, slick well of womanly Eden. He couldn't prevent himself from groaning aloud this time.

He withdrew his hand from her to tear at the fastenings of his pants, struggling to free himself from the restricting fabric. When he fell heavily against her naked hip, the heat and silky texture of her skin was almost more than his aroused body could take. He levered himself over her, settling his weight on her and using his knees to press her legs apart.

When he reached down between them, she allowed him to position her for his entry, her arms still about his neck, her hair a wild halo around her. He tore his mouth from hers as he pressed forward, watching her eyes widen at the same time he felt her body's moist, sweet welcome. He made several shallow forays in and out, his breathing coming in great gasping bellows. Then all control shattered and he pressed himself hard forward, sheathing himself in her until their bodies were pressed together and he was snugly caught.

She jerked involuntarily and a shattered "Oh!" burst from her lips.

He froze. Was she...*had* she been a virgin? He'd never even considered the possibility. And in truth, he couldn't consider it now. He needed to move, and he needed her with him, but he didn't think he was going to be able to wait. "Did I hurt you?" he ground out.

Stupid question. Of course he'd hurt her. He'd just taken her maidenhead with all the finesse of a charging bull.

But then she moved beneath him. Her arms, which had been resting on his biceps, slipped up to his shoulders, gently caressing the taut muscles there. "It's all right. I want you to—go ahead." The words were a mere whisper and he noticed she hadn't answered his question. But his body was screaming for his attention and her permission was a powerful aphrodisiac heightening his urgent arousal. His control, usually an easy part of his sexual experiences, was shredded and fading; he could feel himself already on the edge, each small motion of her tight warm body a sensual torment to his ultra-sensitive flesh. With a muttered apology, he took her hips in his hands and set his mouth on hers, swallowing the sounds she made with his frantic kisses as he plunged in and drew back repeatedly. Her legs came up to clasp his hips and he shuddered as the movement pulled him deeper. And then the storm broke over his head and his back arched in the rhythms of release as his seed jetted deep, deep within her body, until he lay winded and still in the wake of the passing fury.

"Allison." Kane sounded dazed. He lay heavily over her and she kept her arms linked tightly around him, her eyes closed, pressing herself into the amazing heat of his hard body, savoring the moments in which they were physically joined. But then he pulled away from her and all her strength couldn't hold him. She winced at the drag of his flesh against her torn, tender opening, and he made a sound of frustration as he levered himself upright and left her. He stood, looking down at her, hands on hips and all she could do was lie in exhausted silence and take in the magnificence of his sculpted body for the first time.

"Why in *hell* didn't you tell me you were a virgin?" His voice was a low growl. Her eyes shot to his and she shrank from the dark look in those golden depths.

"I didn't think about it," she said in a small voice, shifting a little to ease the discomfort between her thighs. "I was just...feeling."

He snorted, but the ferocious scowl altered into a less forbidding expression. "Yeah," he said. "I know what you mean." His face softened even more, and he reached down and stroked the back of his knuckle down her cheek. "If I'd known, I would have been more gentle."

"You were *perfect,*" she said fiercely. "Quit worrying about it, all right?"

"Not all right." To her astonishment, he bent and slipped his arms beneath her, lifting her up against his bare chest and letting her hair cascade down over his shoulder and arm. He was hot and sweaty and rough with hair, and so exciting that she could feel her toes curl and her abdomen contract, despite the exhaustion that was fast returning.

He held her there a moment, inspecting her face, and then he dropped his head and nuzzled her lips again. "Next time we do this I'll show you how it should have been done."

She couldn't have prevented the smile that broke free as she slipped her arms up around his neck to deepen the light kiss. And when he finally let her breathe again, she said, "Now?"

Kane gave a bark of laughter as he began to walk back

toward the hallway. "For somebody who never let a man—"

"Stop!" She put a palm over his lips. "I was a virgin until a few minutes ago, remember?"

And his smile slipped a notch. His voice held a grim note when he answered her. "I'll never forget."

Kane took her to the bedroom she indicated, surprised somehow by how soft and feminine it was. He didn't know why it surprised him and, remembering earlier when he'd seen her hair down for the first time, he felt vaguely ashamed that he'd misunderstood her so completely. In the workplace she was calm, quiet yet always efficient. He'd thought of her as someone, well, bland, and if he'd ever thought at all about her personal preferences, which he hadn't, he'd have assumed they were quiet and bland as well. In the limited personal moments they'd shared in the past, he realized that she rarely turned the conversation to herself. She'd always encouraged him to talk about himself, and he'd taken full advantage of her generosity.

Now he looked around him with interest, absorbing the ambience, gleaning clues about who the woman in his arms really was. She lay in docile surrender against his chest, her head against his shoulder. As he looked down at her slender body, all he could think was that he never wanted this night to end. Never wanted to have to think of anything but the incredible pleasure her sweet body gave him.

But he *did* have to think of something else. She'd been a virgin. So he knew she wasn't prepared for birth control. And he hadn't given it a damn thought until he'd been so deep inside her there was no chance in hell he could stop. He and Allison could have created a new life.

A child. He wasn't sure how he felt. He'd always known he wanted children, children to whom he could give the kind of childhood he'd never had. But how he felt wasn't really the issue. The issue was that he was an honorable man. His mother had raised him that way, and since he'd met the other members of the Fortune family, he knew where the strong streak of responsibility came from. Rarely did a Fortune walk away from his responsibilities.

He thought of his mother, a teenager with twin infants, totally overwhelmed and alone in a strange city. She'd been sure her father would never accept her back again, pregnant and unmarried. Maybe some people would see it as a shirking of responsibilities, but he thought it was the ultimate act of honor to give up children for whom she knew she couldn't provide, to hope that they'd be adopted by loving families with adequate resources that she hadn't had.

Well, he had the resources. And no child of his would ever be given away. The woman in his arms could very well be carrying his child after this night so he'd marry her. *He'd marry her.* The solution was so simple! They'd get married as soon as he could arrange it.

He wasn't going to have people counting backward on their fingers and coming up with the wrong conclusions. He'd been the butt of gossip much of his life, one way or another. No child of his was going to have to suffer the cruel talk he had.

You don't really have a dad, do you? I bet your mom was never married at all. He forced his mind away from the remembered taunts. No, his child would never have to endure anything like that.

It was a good solution in more ways than one, he realized as he looked down at the woman in his arms. He couldn't even begin to imagine the reasons that she might still have been a virgin at her age. But it couldn't have been a casual choice. No, if Allison had given herself to him after so many years of chastity, then he had an obligation to treat her gift as the special treasure it had been.

Besides, he was thirty years old. Nothing would please his mother more than to have him settled and giving her grandchildren to spoil.

And she'd like Allison. No, she'd probably *love* Allison. She'd take one look and see the gentle, selfless spirit, the honesty and integrity, the bone-deep kindness that radiated from Allison, and she'd see what he saw: the perfect woman with whom to spend his life. Satisfaction filled him. He could already imagine her soothing presence in his home and he liked the image. He liked it a lot.

And Allison would be a wonderful mother for his children. He already knew she would be great with infants since he'd seen the careful tenderness with which she handled babies in the neonatal unit. She was soft and sweet, easygoing yet competent. He couldn't find a better-suited woman to mother his children if he tried.

She shifted in his arms and as he pulled his thoughts back to the present, he saw apprehension fill her gaze before she looked away. She swallowed. "Thank you," she said, raising a hand and gently cupping his cheek. "I won't…won't make this more than it was. I don't want to make you feel obligated or uncomfortable."

He arched an eyebrow. "Is that so?"

"No." She rushed on. "It's not as if—"

"Allison."

She stopped, and her gaze came back to his.

"It's too bad if you don't want me to feel obligated because that's exactly how I want you to feel."

She hesitated, and he thought she might be holding her breath. "Meaning?"

"Meaning I want you to marry me."

"*What?*" Her expression was so shocked he almost laughed.

"Marry me."

She began to struggle in his arms and he pivoted, sitting on the edge of the bed and cradling her in his lap, controlling her until she stopped moving and lay against him again, her head on his shoulder, face turned up to his with a bewildered expression.

"Tonight…" he said. "Sex isn't a casual thing for you. And we didn't use birth control. I could have gotten you pregnant."

"But…you don't have to—you can't marry me!" She looked completely panicked, her body stiff and uncomfortable against his.

"I know I don't have to. I want to." He dropped his head and sought her mouth, kissing her with deep intent until she was limp and pliant in his embrace and her arms came up to clutch at his neck as she returned his kisses. Then he lifted his head. "Say yes."

She gazed at him for a long time, then closed her eyes. "You're crazy. You'd hate being married to me."

The flat certainty in her tone took him aback, but he noticed she hadn't said *she'd* hate being married to *him*. "I've thought about it," he told her, his hand slipping down to cover a breast, "and I wouldn't hate it at all. I think we're well suited. We're great in bed and we get along well outside it, too."

She blushed. "Those aren't solid reasons to get married." But she didn't push his hand away.

"They're better than some. Think about it," he urged, a sense of urgency rushing through him, "and you'll see I'm right. How many other men do you talk to the way we've talked?"

She was silent.

A new thought occurred to him. Were there other men whom she'd treated as sweetly and gently as she'd treated him in the course of their friendship? The idea didn't set well. "How many other men—?" he began, but she cut him off.

"None," she said. "But, Kane, I just don't think you've really thought this through. You're a Fortune."

"Who cares what my last name is?" Dammit, what was wrong with her? She *had* to marry him. "Say yes," he prompted, his fingers shaping her nipple, tugging and rolling the taut flesh, teasing himself as much as he was teasing her. "We'll be good together. And if you're pregnant, I'll be delighted."

Her eyes drooped, closed. She hesitated, then took a deep breath. "Yes."

He thought she sounded more like she was agreeing to an execution than a wedding, but the relief that swamped him was so intense and unexpected that he couldn't comment. What was going on here? It was only that she was so perfect for the role, he decided. He'd have to look a long time to find another woman who fit so well into his life. And he had neither the time nor the inclination to go wife-hunting.

He lifted her again, turned to the pretty spindle bed and laid her down, taking the time to spread her hair out over the pillow. Then he went to the bathroom he'd passed and found a washcloth, running it beneath warm water before he returned to the bedroom.

He was amused to see that she'd pulled a sheet over herself and even more amused that she protested when he tugged it away and began to clean her. "I'm going to be looking at you every day soon," he said, "So you might as well put the modesty in the past."

"I can't," she said, covering her face with her hands, and he chuckled, setting the washcloth aside.

"This hair," he murmured, moving onto the mattress beside her and pulling her into his arms as he buried his face in the fragrant mass. "I can't believe you hid this hair from me for four years."

Allison didn't speak, though he felt her smile against his throat. She'd said very little since they'd risen from the couch, and he had a moment's sudden panic that he'd hurt her badly, even though she'd just agreed to marry him. He leaned over her, cupping the sweet weight of one breast in his hand again and absently brushing his thumb across the tip. "Are you sure you're all right? I was too rough."

"I'm okay," she said, and once again that light wash of color stole up her cheeks.

He grinned. "How can you still blush?"

Now there were bright flags of color painting her complexion. "I don't know," she said helplessly, looking everywhere but at him.

"You know," he said, his voice deepening in anticipation, "There are a lot more things we could do if you *really* want something to blush about."

He'd expected her to hide her face in his shoulder and laugh, but instead, her green eyes fastened on his, filled with interest and rising desire. "Show me."

His whole body leaped to attention. Relief rushed through him as he realized he really hadn't hurt her, hadn't frightened her, despite the lack of care he'd taken and the way he'd left her behind in his pursuit of fulfillment. This time, he thought, he'd make sure she was with him all the way. And he'd do it all for her.

So he did, pressing her back against the pillows and kissing his way over her from earlobe to tiny pink toe, sucking and nipping, running his tongue along the backs of her sensitive knees and then moving up to stroke and suckle her beautiful breasts. He smoothed his hands from her shoulders down to her wrists, then twined his fingers with hers and lifted them above her head, anchoring them there with one hand while he continued to explore her with the other. After a long while, he knelt near her feet and spread her legs, holding them apart with strong hands when she murmured a protest. And then the protests turned to moans as he kissed a path up the inside of one leg, slipping steadily up and up, lingering over the satiny flesh of her inner thighs, until finally, finally he put his mouth over her. He tasted her gently, inhaling her fragrant female scent. His tongue sought out the tiny pouting bump hidden within the damp blond curls, laving it gently until she was writhing beneath his mouth. Suddenly, he increased both the pressure and the rhythm and she arched and cried out as her body convulsed and she shook with her own release.

When she was calm again, he slipped up to gather her into his arms, nestling her head beneath his chin. *"That,"* he said, "was how it should have been for your first time." He couldn't change that, much to his regret. But the thought stole into his mind that after they married, this sweet, responsive, incredibly passionate woman would be in his bed every night, and the idea filled him with pleasure.

"That was…wonderful," she breathed. Then her small hand drifted over his chest and down his belly, hovering a breath away from his taut, swollen flesh. "But you haven't—you need to—" She stopped, and he figured if he looked, he'd see pink cheeks again.

"Any man who tells you he *needs* to is a damn liar."

She laughed, as he'd intended. But then her eyes grew serious and her fingers traced small circles around his navel. "It's your turn now."

He inhaled sharply, drawing her hand away. "I can't,"

he said. "I'm not the kind of guy who carries protection around in his wallet. We already took one chance…"

"I don't think it's the right time for conception," she said. "Besides, if we did…um, make a baby, it would be all right."

His body leaped at her words, but still he hesitated. "I don't have to." He was reluctant to overwhelm her, even though his throbbing loins were calling his bluff in a most obvious way.

"What if I want you to?" Her voice was shy and so was the gentle hand that settled on him, but he jumped like a scalded cat and then groaned, relaxing into her.

"My mother raised a gentleman," he reminded her. "I guess I can't refuse a lady's request."

She stifled a giggle. "Gee, that was hard."

"No," he corrected her, rolling to his back and pulling her against his side, "*this* is hard." He taught her how to stroke him, wrapping his hand around hers and showing her the speed and pressure that he liked. After her first few moments of tentative exploration, she got so good at what she was doing that he finally had to grab her hand and stop her before he lost it completely. Again.

"Wait," he said in a strangled tone.

"Why?" Her voice was apprehensive and her hand stopped moving.

"Because I'm going to finish this right here, right now if you don't."

She took her hand away and he almost whimpered at the cessation of the hot, sweet pleasure coursing through him. "I liked the way you finished it before," she told his throat.

He angled himself enough to peer down at her face, his body leaping at the mere suggestion. "The first time?"

She nodded, her eyes still on his throat. She was so shy, he thought with a touch of tender amusement.

He traced her jawbone and dropped his head to press a gentle kiss on her lips. This time she didn't need to be coaxed to open her legs. This time, he held her gaze with his, looking intimately into her eyes as he slid his hard, hungry length into her receptive body and began to move, holding the eye contact as he felt the tremors of release scampering up his spine. He reached down between them and found her, gently rubbing and rolling her between his thumb and forefinger and her eyes widened in shock. Her mouth opened and she cried out, and as they both began to shudder in the final moments of the dance of completion, he sealed his mouth over hers and drank the sweet cries from her lips.

Allison's alarm clock chirped a wake-up call at dawn. She'd slept in his arms through the night, and he'd woken several times to the novel sensation of sleeping with someone. It was surprisingly enjoyable even though it wasn't something he was accustomed to. A doctor in training didn't have time to sleep, much less think about sex.

But he was thinking about it now. Oh, was he ever!

Allison stirred when the alarm went off, reaching out a hand to turn it off. Still half asleep, he put a hand on her bare shoulder and she turned to him easily, letting him pull her down beneath him and slide into her, the soft wet depths of her body welcoming and already familiar. Hips pumping steadily, he rode her in a relaxed, easy rhythm that nonetheless stoked the fires that slumbered inside him. He took her legs and wrapped them around his waist, angling her hips up so that he was arousing her with each stroke, and when she started to whimper and buck beneath him, he let himself come to her, long slow streamers of release melting his bones and leaving him slumped on her equally limp body.

"Good morning," he said into her ear when he'd gotten his breath back.

"Good morning." There was a lilt in her voice.

"Today," he said, his voice grim as he came awake enough to remember what he'd forgotten, "I'm going to start using birth control."

She smiled up at him, her eyes sparkling as her hands massaged the muscles at the back of his neck. "Nothing like closing the barn door after the horse is out." Then she turned her head and looked at the clock again, and immediately her small hands began shoving at his shoulders. "Get up! I've got to get moving or I'll be late! I'm on dayshift today."

He complied, rolling off her to lie on his back until she was out of the shower. He took a quick shower after her, and by the time he walked back into the bedroom, she was dressed and was brushing her hair with quick, hard strokes. As she pulled it tightly back and began to wind it into its usual confined style, he walked over to stand behind her and put his hands on her shoulders, looking into her eyes in the mirror.

"Are you about ready to go?"

She nodded, turning to the mirror and pushing a few more pins into her hair. "Almost."

He was distracted by the small, feminine ritual as he watched her tuck up her hair. "I'm glad you wear it up at work," he said. "I don't like the thought of anyone else seeing all that hair and getting ideas."

Her hands stilled in her hair and she turned to stare at him, clearly dumbfounded. Hell, he knew how she felt. Someone he didn't know had just stepped into his head and uttered words he hadn't expected to come out of his own mouth.

He cleared his throat. "Let's go."

* * *

Allison floated through her shift on autopilot, doing all her usual tasks with her usual efficiency, but her mind was back in her bedroom.

I want you to marry me.

When she went into the supply closet for something, she actually pinched herself. This couldn't be real.

Yesterday, she'd been a plain single nurse with both her virginity and a hopeless crush on the hottest doctor in the whole hospital. Today…in whomever's dream this was, she was marrying him. And she wasn't a virgin anymore.

For years, celibacy had been a conscious choice. She'd expected to marry and give her husband the gift of her body. But the years had drifted by and love had never found her. Until Kane. And though she hadn't known he would marry her, when he'd begun to caress her she'd realized immediately that this man and this moment were what she'd wanted for so many years. Kane had made love to her. To *her*. He'd marked every inch of her with his stamp—she had brush burns from his beard in some pretty darned intimate places!—and he hadn't just done it once, either. He'd lingered over her, made sure that she was as satisfied as he was. He'd done wonderful things to her that she'd remember for the rest of her life.

The world was a very crazy place. And she was equally insane, to be standing here dreaming about a wedding and a life with a man like Kane Fortune. One of *the* Fortunes.

Kane wasn't really going to marry her, no matter how hard her heart beat at the thought. He'd gotten brusque and abrupt as they'd met in the parking lot after the brief drive and walked toward the hospital doors together. He was probably regretting his offer already.

Well, she would be gracious. Treat it as if he'd been joking. That way she wouldn't lose him as a friend. She didn't think she could bear it if he avoided her, didn't want her friendship and left her with nothing. Not after they'd been so close.

She was in the lounge later, checking through the refrigerator to see if there was any creamer that didn't have things growing in or on it, when Kane came through the door. He looked tired and harried, and the circles that had been beneath his eyes last night were even worse than before. He hadn't gotten enough sleep, and it was her fault—

"Hi. You off at seven?" He busied himself pouring a cup of coffee.

"Yes." She braced herself. Already, she thought. From his manner she could tell he was uncomfortable, and an arrow of hurt sliced through her heart.

"It'll be too late tonight, but if you're off tomorrow we can go pick out rings." His words were casual, but he eyed her over the rim of his cup as he took a sip, narrowing his eyes against either the steam or the lousy taste, she wasn't sure which.

"It's the start of my weekend," she began. Then his words registered. "Rings? Are you sure you want to do this? Kane, you know I don't expect you to marry me on the slim chance that I might have gotten…that I might have conceived. Why don't we wait a few weeks and see? There might not even be a reason to get married."

"Oh, there's a reason." He set down his coffee cup and crossed the lounge, reaching out to place his hands at her hips and pull her toward him. "Allison, I know you. If you were still a virgin at the age of—how old are you, anyway?"

"Twenty-six," she supplied.

"—twenty-six, then you had a reason. You didn't give yourself to me casually." He pulled her closer and his voice deepened. "You committed yourself to me the first time I got inside you and neither of us used protection, baby. The second time, and the third, just added a little weight to it.'' He slipped his arms around her and pressed her hips against his with a short, frustrated laugh and her body thrilled to his touch. ''The only choice you have to make now is whether or not you want to use birth control from here on out on the off chance we aren't going to be parents right away.''

He was serious. And even though she understood him now, knew that his own fatherless childhood must have made him determined not to make the same mistake with a child of his own, she found it difficult to breathe, her body suffused with a glowing heat at his frank words and the pressure of his aroused male body growing against her. He was really serious about getting married. *To her!*

She looked up into his beautiful golden eyes, sliding her hands up his chest and daring to smooth them out across the heavy muscles of his shoulders. ''All right.'' She took a deep breath. ''Maybe we should use protection at first. We can decide later when we want children…if it hasn't already been decided for us by the fertility gods.''

''That's fine with me.'' Kane dropped his head to kiss her—

And at that exact instant, the door to the lounge opened and two of the other nursing staff started in.

''Oh my God!'' said one, clearly too shocked to be tactful.

The taller woman just grinned, her eyebrows raised in surprise. ''Hey, Dr. Fortune, where do we get in line?''

''Sorry, no line,'' said Kane, smiling at the two women. His fingers bit into Allison's ribs and his arms were inflexible bands of steel holding her imprisoned against him as she tried discreetly to put some distance between them.

"But you can be the first to congratulate us on our upcoming marriage."

Allison would have laughed at the thunderstruck faces of her coworkers if she hadn't been embarrassed enough to sink through the floor. "Kane!"

"What?" His look was pure innocence. "When you come in with a ring, don't you think people are going to start to wonder?"

The other two women were open-mouthed with shock. Allison could only imagine what they were thinking. Probably the same thing that kept sneaking through her own mind. *What's a hunk like Dr. Fortune doing with a plain little thing like Allison Preston?*

Congratulations were passed around and the two women backed out the door of the lounge without ever coming in. Kane waited until the door was closed before he released her.

"I guess this isn't the time or the place for romance." He walked across the room and lifted his coffee mug. "I'll pick you up after your shift ends tonight and we'll go out to my place. I'd like you to see it, decide if it suits you or if we should look for something else."

And before she could agree, disagree or simply start tearing her hair out, Kane came over, casually kissed the tip of her nose and walked out of the lounge. She stared after him, one hand going up to touch her nose. Was she crazy or was he?

Three

—

"**Y**ou're *what?*" His mother's eyebrows appeared about to take wing and fly right off her lovely face.

Kane snorted at her obvious shock. "I'm getting married. Surprised?"

Miranda slowly shook her head, smiling wryly. "Not really. You've always kept the most important things in your life to yourself until you had all your plans made."

"Like what?" Was that true?

His mother held up one finger. "Like when you were fourteen and you started your own lawn-care business to save money for college because you'd decided you wanted to be a doctor. I found out when the bank needed a legal guardian's name on your savings account." She held up a second finger. "Like when you were sixteen and you applied for the volunteer program at the hospital because you wanted it on your resumé. You told me *after* you'd gotten into the program." Yet a third finger joined the first two.

"And when you applied to med school, no one ever heard a peep about it until you'd been accepted."

"Okay. Point made." Kane held up a hand. An unexpected pang of guilt shot through him. He'd never looked at it from his mother's angle. It was just that he hated to fail, and he preferred not to blab all his hopes and dreams aloud. He'd chosen not to bother his mother with his problems through most of his life, because she'd already been dealing with so much. To him, it made perfect sense not to make a fuss over possibilities until they were realities. That way, no one's hopes got dashed but his if things fell through.

The truth was, it simply never occurred to him to confide in other people. Except for Allison. He was still amazed at how easily she had fit into his life. He could hardly wait until they were married.

"So tell me about her," his mother prompted.

"She's blond. She has green eyes."

His mother rolled her own eyes. "Honestly, Kane, sometimes I can't imagine that I raised you! Where did you meet? How long have you known each other?"

"Her name is Allison. Allison Preston. She's a nurse. I met her four years ago when she started working in the peds unit at County. We've been friends since then, but I didn't get smart enough to stake a claim until recently." Well, that was true. "She's quiet, very sweet, sort of shy. You'll want to mother her."

"Is she from San Antonio?"

"Yes." *I think.*

"Does she have family here?"

"No." At least, he didn't think she did. But she'd never really spoken of her family. In fact, when he really thought about it, she'd never told him much at all about herself. *Because you're always too busy talking about yourself, maybe?* It was an uncomfortably accurate thought, and a rather disturbing one, when he contrasted it to the way he'd deliberately held on to his privacy with his own family members.

"Look," he said, anxious to distract his mother, "She gets off work at seven and we're having dinner at my house. How about if I bring her by for a few minutes around nine so you can meet her?"

Kane stood in his kitchen, a glass of wine in his hand. After the visit with his mother, he'd picked up Allison and brought her straight out here to his home and now she was changing out of her nursing things into casual clothes. He wondered if she'd let down her hair again.

If she didn't, he was going to have to do it for her.

Ruefully, he shook his head. How in the hell could he have gotten so obsessed about one woman and her sexy hair in the space of less than two days? He'd had a tough time concentrating all day long because every second that he wasn't busy, he was remembering how it felt to slide into her tight wet depths, the little noises she'd made when she came, the feel of her small, soft hands on his decidedly not small, hard—

The kitchen was definitely not the place for the kind of reaction his body was giving his thoughts.

This would stop. Surely this would stop soon, after the initial flush of sexual intimacy faded. Although right now he couldn't even imagine being immune to her charm, let alone apathetic about making love to her.

Why did she affect him so strongly? It wasn't as if she were a raving beauty. But she had a quiet sweetness, he quickly amended. A gentle sparkle of warmth and humor that someone would have to nurture to enjoy. That *he* would enjoy from now on. Thinking about her, he realized that she *did* have a quiet kind of beauty that he'd simply overlooked in the past.

It wasn't just that hair and the sex he'd thought about all day, if he were honest with himself. And it wasn't even the amazingly pretty body beneath the shapeless uniforms in which he usually saw her. Her profile was delicate, her little nose so straight and cute he hadn't been able to resist kissing it earlier. Her skin was fine-grained and satiny all over, her eyebrows arched and surprisingly dark for a natural blonde, while equally dark, flirtatiously long lashes often concealed the thoughts going on in her head. Though she was the farthest thing from a flirt he'd ever met and she'd probably die if he told her what one look from beneath those lashes did to him. Aside from her glorious tresses, her eyes were definitely her prettiest feature, though, wide and greener than any he'd ever seen, with a dark rim around the iris that enhanced their color. Then again, when she smiled...

He honestly couldn't figure out why he'd never noticed her before, even if she wasn't his usual type.

And then she came into the room, and he knew.

She made herself invisible. Quiet, self-effacing, unassuming, those were the words that sprang to mind, but she carried them to such an extreme that she practically melted into the wallpaper. It was one of the things that had drawn him to her in the first place, because he'd found her presence to be so soothing and restful that after a short break talking to her in the cafeteria, he was almost always less uptight and in a better mood.

And damned if he wasn't still obsessing about her! *This had to stop.*

"You look nice," he said, enjoying the sight of her legs beneath the short white skirt, and the swell of her breasts under the pink top that matched the color that rose in her cheeks. Though the clothing wasn't too revealing or deliberately provocative, he could immediately feel his interest level revving up. If that were possible.

"So," he said. "I thought we'd eat dinner first and then I'd like to take you to meet my mother."

"Your mother!" She wasn't invisible anymore. His words had rattled her, and she stared at him wide-eyed, shaking her head until her shining curls danced. "I'm not dressed to meet your mother. Do I have to?"

He laughed. She sounded genuinely panicked. "Yes, you have to. Stop worrying, you look fine. I stopped by today and told her I was getting married. She'll cut off my ear if I don't introduce you right away."

"Oh. Well, I guess we can't have you earless." She looked around his kitchen, obviously at a loss for words.

"So what do you think of my home? I know there's not a lot of furniture yet, but that'll happen eventually. My school loans are finally paid off, and a mortgage was all the debt I was willing to assume when the place was built." He waited, unwilling to acknowledge his interest in her reaction.

Maybe she wouldn't like it. It was awfully spartan, and that wasn't simply due to a lack of funds. It never occurred to him to decorate his living quarters. After all, who would see it but him?

Allison looked around the kitchen, walking over to stand at the French doors that opened onto a patio with a sparkling blue pool at the far end. Then she turned and her eyes were shining. "I love it, Kane. Your whole home is beautiful, furniture or not."

"Good." He ignored the rush of relief her words brought. "I worked with the architect, and I'm pleased with the end result. And there are five bedrooms in addition to the master suite so there's plenty of room for children."

The mention of children brought that delicate hint of color slipping back up her cheeks. It was absolutely... adorable. Enticing. And he hoped like hell the day never came when he couldn't make her blush.

"Children," she said, and he wondered if she knew her voice almost ached with longing and wonder. "I still can't believe this."

"You might find it easier to believe in nine months."

"It would seem funny, holding a full-term healthy baby," she said. "I'm so used to the preemies."

"I know." To distract her from the sober topic of their occupations, he idly asked, "Have you ever thought about how many children you'd like to have?"

Her answering smile was soft and dreamy, and her eyes looked past him to something he couldn't picture. "One for each bedroom, at least."

His whole body reacted to the thought of all the time they'd have to spend creating five children. He crossed to her and handed her a glass of wine, then slipped his hand behind her head, threading his fingers through the heavy mass of her hair and tilting her face up to his. "That's a lot of children."

Her brow wrinkled and she searched his eyes. "Too many?" Her whole face fell. "You're right. I—"

He stopped the oncoming rush of words by putting his mouth on hers and thrusting his tongue deep into her mouth. She sagged against him, putting her free arm up around his shoulders. He immediately gathered her hard to him, automatically aligning her soft curves with his body, and they both groaned at the feel of the intimate position.

He lifted his mouth a fraction. "I didn't say I didn't want a lot of kids," he clarified. "I think a houseful would be great."

Her eyes lit up, glowing emerald with happiness, and he flexed his fingers on her soft hips.

"You don't have to work tomorrow, do you?"

She shook her head slightly, her eyes focusing on him. "No. I'm off for the next three days."

"Good." He kissed her once more, then released her. "You're staying tonight. Tomorrow we'll start moving your things in and you can give up your lease."

Her eyebrows rose. "You don't believe in rushing things, do you?"

He shrugged. "There's no reason to wait."

"And you also don't believe in asking." But she was smiling a little.

"Sorry. Comes from years of giving medical orders, I guess."

"Uh-huh. You can't fool me. You were born like this."

He grimaced. "You're going to get along well with my sister."

She looked panicked again. "Will she be there tonight, too?" He could almost see her wilting at the thought.

"No, just my mother. We'll save my sister for another day."

But she was still looking troubled. "How are you going to explain this?"

"Explain what?" She was looking up at him with wide, sad eyes and he had the strongest urge to simply take her in his arms and cuddle her.

"You know." She spoke slowly, as if he were missing an important point. "This. This…*us.*"

He didn't have a clue. "What are you talking about?"

Her face grew serious. "Kane, are you really that dense?" She sighed. "You're a handsome charming man, a doctor. A member of the Fortune family. No one will ever believe I'm the kind of woman you would marry.

I'm…'' She gestured helplessly. "I'm not a model or an actress, or a socialite. Or any kind of special woman." She tried to turn away from him but he gripped her waist and held her so she had to face him. Still, she turned her head away.

He didn't know what to say for a minute. "You think just because my last name is Fortune I have to marry some woman who's…who's *famous* in some way?"

She bit her lip. "You know what I mean."

"No," he said in a tone that brooked no interruption. "I do not. My mother was an actress wannabe who waitressed for twenty years. My cousin married the daughter of my uncle's housekeeper. My sister married a cop. Well, a sheriff, it's almost the same thing." He took her chin in his hand and forced her to look at him again. "Sounds like you're a backward sort of snob."

"I am not!"

He had to chuckle at the vehemence in her tone. "I've never seen it before, if you are," he said quietly. "I see a woman with a glow that lights her up from the inside out. A woman with beautiful eyes and a smile that can make a man feel as if she thinks he's the most important thing in her universe—"

"You worked with me for four years without really noticing me," she pointed out.

"Yeah, and now I'm thinking I must have been taking stupid pills," he muttered, frustrated that he didn't seem to be getting through.

It was just an offhand comment, but her eyes lit up and her hesitant, pretty smile turned up the drooping corners of her lips as if he'd sung an ode to her beauty.

"This," Kane announced, as he pulled up in front of a beautifully landscaped villa, "is Melrose Manor."

"Melrose Manor? You're kidding. Like the TV show a few years back?"

He nodded. "My mother's got a weird sense of humor."

They walked up the wide flagstone path to the door but before Kane could reach for the doorknob, the wide double doors flew open. "It's about time you got here!"

The speaker was a slim, shapely blonde who looked far too young to be Kane's mother. But the family resemblance was strong, though their coloring was different.

"Mother, I'd like you to meet Allison Preston. My fiancée."

Allison held out her hand and it was promptly clasped between two warm palms. "Hello, Allison. It's wonderful to meet you. I'm Miranda. Please come in." Miranda Fortune fairly bubbled with energy.

She led the way through a flagstone entry hall into a pretty sitting room, where she promptly turned and embraced Kane. "Thank you for bringing her. Now go away so we can talk."

"So you can interrogate her, you mean." He grinned easily. "Not a chance." He reached out and took Allison's hand. "She's twenty-six, she has all her teeth and I'm marrying her before you can scare her off. That's all you need to know."

They all laughed and, after they'd sat down, she offered them drinks. Miranda was charming, and so unpretentious Allison could hardly believe she was one of the wealthiest women in the country.

But after a few moments of general getting-to-know-you chat, Kane cleared his throat. When both women paused and looked at him, he addressed his mother. "Have you heard anything more from Carter?"

"I—uh, no." Miranda looked taken aback and Allison

realized it was because Kane was discussing such an intimate family matter in front of a near stranger.

"Could you show me where the powder room is?" She rose but Kane took her hand and pulled her back down onto the loveseat beside him.

"Mother, she knows about your...the phone call."

Miranda's eyes widened, then she turned to Allison. "Please, you must understand how important it is to keep this quiet—"

"I wouldn't have told her if she were a gossip, Mother." Kane stood, resting his hand on Allison's shoulder. "We have no secrets, but you don't have to worry that anyone will learn yours from Allison."

Allison dropped her eyes. No, they didn't exactly have secrets. Mentally, she slammed the door on the brief glimpse of her past that peeked through. There was nothing there to remember. Nothing.

"You really must be close to Kane," Miranda was saying. She shook her finger at him. "I cannot believe you hid this girl away until you were engaged! We could have been getting to know each other."

Allison shifted uncomfortably as she smiled at Kane's pretty mother. But before she could speak, Kane said, "You know I've never been good at sharing. Our time together is limited because of our schedules, and I like having her all to myself."

Before he could really get going, Allison placed a restraining hand on his arm and addressed Miranda Fortune. "I'm sorry to hear about your difficulties. Have you decided what you're going to do?"

Kane's mother's face fell. She sighed, twisting her elegant hands together. "I keep hoping that if I ignore the whole thing, it'll just go away." She paused and then looked squarely at Allison. "Has Kane told you everything?"

He nodded before she could speak.

A tear slipped down Miranda's cheek. "I didn't intend that anyone should ever know."

"I seriously doubt that ignoring this is going to make it go away." Kane's voice was harsh and his fingers grew tight around hers. Wincing, Allison laid a soothing hand on his, stroking his knuckles absently with her fingertips as she listened to the exchange.

"Have you told Uncle Ryan yet?"

"No." Miranda began to cry silently. "I can barely think about it, much less talk about it. And I'm quite sure he knows the twins' father socially. He'll be so shocked."

"You have to," Kane said firmly though he looked equally disturbed. "And then you have to go to the police. Blackmail is illegal."

Allison was shaken by the realization that Miranda's long-ago lover apparently still lived in the area.

"No! We can't involve the police. I've done enough to blacken the Fortune family name in my life; I won't drag all of you through the kind of publicity that would generate." She lifted her hands in a helpless, hopeless gesture. "I guess I'm going to have to pay Lloyd. If I refuse, he'll go straight to..." Her voice started to hitch and Allison moved automatically, putting her arms around the stricken woman. "And I just couldn't face him. He'd never forgive me."

Driving home from his mother's a short time later, Kane said, "If you don't want my mother to mess in the wedding plans, tell me now."

"No, no," she said hastily. "I'd love to have your mother's help."

"Will your mother want to be involved?"

The question caught her off guard. "My mother's dead," she finally said.

"I'm sorry," he said after a moment of silence had passed. "I didn't realize."

"It's all right." She worked to steady her voice. "She had some health problems, and she caught pneumonia a couple of years ago in the hospital."

He grimaced. "The disgrace of the medical profession. Send people to the hospital to be healed, and they get pneumonia."

She nodded. "Exactly." There was a small silence but she spoke into it before he could ask any more questions about her family. "So I'd welcome your mother's help."

"Help." She heard his sarcastic snort as he repeated the word. "It'll be more like we're the asphalt and she's the steamroller. We'll be saying 'I do' before you know what hit you."

Saying, "I do…" Privately, Allison still couldn't believe Kane truly intended them to marry. This couldn't be happening to her.

But it was. And the moment Kane got her home, he demonstrated just how real it was, taking her straight to bed. He dragged the pins from her hair and plunged his hands into her tidy knot, pulling the heavy mass into a tangle of free-flowing tresses. He stripped away first her clothing and then his, and laid her down on his enormous bed and covered her with his body, taking time only to use the protection he'd finally bought that afternoon.

Allison wrapped her arms and legs around him as he entered her urgently, wonder dissolving into ecstasy as she gave herself fully to his demands. His intensity lit a similar frantic need within her as well, and within minutes, they found a wrenching satisfaction. But unlike the first night,

Kane rolled away from her immediately, lying with an arm flung over his eyes.

The action startled and dismayed her. He almost seemed to be radiating Do Not Disturb signals, and she felt naked and exposed, so she pulled the sheet over herself and lay quietly beside him, wondering what to do or say. Had she done something wrong? Or was he bored with her already? There was a palpable tension in the air and though she longed to ask him what was wrong, it was clear that he didn't want to talk. It bothered her increasingly until she thought she might scream if the silence wasn't broken soon.

Finally, with a huge sigh, Kane removed his arm from over his eyes. He reached for her, seeming surprised at the sheet between them, and pulled her into his arms. Then he flipped the light covers up over them both. "Go to sleep," he said gruffly.

Something still felt wrong, but he was holding her, cuddling her against him and she felt better almost against her will. She was tired after working her four days, and before she knew it, her eyelids drifted closed and she slept.

Kane lay in the darkness, and a feeling very close to desperation swept through him. The small woman in his arms was driving him insane. What was it about her that he suddenly couldn't stop thinking about? He'd hustled her out of his mother's early because he couldn't wait to have her again, and when they'd walked through the door of his home, he'd fallen on her like a starving wolf on a fresh kill. This insatiable sexual appetite, this *neediness,* wasn't something he'd ever experienced before. It wasn't a comfortable feeling, and he didn't like it. Didn't like it at all. If they'd been at her house, he'd have gotten up and left afterward, reclaimed some of the personal space he seemed to have lost since last night when she'd caught him with his defenses down. At least, it was comforting to tell himself that's what he would have done.

He looked down at her, asleep in the circle of his arms. Her hair spilled over him, chaining him in place, and the scent of her soap mingled with the musky, after-sex fragrance that was uniquely hers, and he could feel himself growing aroused again.

But he didn't move, didn't caress and claim her as he longed to do. They said denial was good for the soul and he might as well start improving his right now, because he damn well wasn't going to be ruled by his hormones or the brain in his pants that frequently argued with the one in his head. Ever since he'd been very small, he'd had to be the strong one, the member of his family on whom the others had leaned.

Not the one who needed to lean.

Gabrielle had depended on him to care for her after school until their mother had got home from work. He'd found a part-time job as soon as he was old enough so that his mother wouldn't have to worry about where his college education was coming from. Even after his mother had decided to move back here to San Antonio to be near Gabrielle, her husband, Wyatt, and their new daughter, she'd been hesitant to make the move without him. Not because she couldn't take care of herself, but because it had become second nature for her to turn to Kane before making any major decisions. And so he'd looked into getting a residency here at County, and he'd joined her, building a home close enough to be nearby without being too obvious about it.

He'd never needed anyone to coddle him in his life. And just because he thought he could get all too used to being cared for and fussed over by Allison didn't mean he was going to let that happen. He despised himself for the weakness he'd shown, whining to her about his family problems, and he was determined not to do it again.

The next morning, he did rounds and let her sleep in.

It was an odd feeling to walk out of his house knowing she was asleep in his bed, recalling the way her hair spilled over his pillow, her lips parted slightly in utter relaxation. He'd gone in to say goodbye before he'd left, just as a courtesy to let her know he was leaving. But when he'd sat down on the edge of the mattress, she'd reached up for him and the sheet fell away from her breasts. He found himself pressing her back against the pillows as he fondled her soft flesh, his mouth deepening the light kiss he'd intended to give her as he'd skimmed one hand down over her silky curves to cup her bottom.

It had been a toss-up there for a minute as to whether he would make love to her again or leave her, but then he remembered his resolve not to be ruled by his gonads so he'd disentangled himself and gotten the hell out of there before he made a fool of himself again.

It was an uneventful day at the hospital. He finished by early afternoon and returned to the house, where Allison was up and about by now. She made him a quick lunch, and then he took her to a jewelry store in the North Star Mall his cousin Vanessa had recommended several years ago when he'd bought his mother a necklace as a Christmas gift.

Allison was hesitant about choosing rings but after he picked out several and made her try them on, she finally chose a contemporary set, a solitaire with a matching wedding band that slid over it and locked it into place. It looked classy and elegant on her long fingers and as he looked at it, he imagined those fingers on his body, doing the things he'd so recently taught her. His body's immediate response was predictable and annoying, and he vowed he wouldn't give in to thoughts of sex one more time today.

She bought a simple gold wedding band for him as well, and then they drove to her apartment and began packing her things to move into his house. She was reluctant to let him work at first, but when he made her see he wasn't going to go away, she told him to start in the living room while she packed her clothes.

Kane boxed her CDs and her stereo system, smiling at the rock 'n' roll classics that predated her birth. Then he moved on to three shelves of books, again surprised at the kinds of things she'd chosen to keep. She appeared to love science fiction and had extensive collections of nearly a dozen different authors on the same shelves with nursing textbooks and a non-fiction historical section largely centered around the Civil War. Although he was beginning to realize that his bride-to-be was a much more complex person than he'd suspected, he still didn't really have a clue about what made her tick.

Why did she work so hard to hide her light under the proverbial basket? Underneath her buttoned-down exterior was a woman who loved to let her hair fly free, who drove an eye-popping red, fun little car, who enjoyed rock music and fantastic stories. A woman who responded so passionately to his touch that he could hardly imagine she'd kept her sensuality hidden from him for four years.

He carefully wrapped a stunning collection of over two dozen miniature crystal cats done by a very well-known jeweler who specialized in crystal miniatures. When she walked through to the kitchen once for a drink, he held one up. "This is quite a collection. Have you had them long?"

Allison had her back to him. "Oh, yes." She stretched on tiptoe to get down two glasses. "There's one for each year of my life."

"Gifts?"

She nodded, concentrating on filling the glasses with ice and water, then walking across to offer him one. "My father started it when he bought the first one on the day I was born. He gave me one each year on my birthday."

She'd said her parents were divorced, and he'd had the impression that her father had disappeared from her life. But he must have been wrong. As she returned to her own packing in the bedroom, he continued carefully wrapping each of the cat figurines in a thick padding of tissue. Her father must have cared for her a great deal, to have kept up with a collection like that for all these years.

And then he found the photos. In a cardboard box in the bottom of a sideboard in the dining room, shoved back behind a beautiful set of antique wineglasses, was a shoebox. He pulled it out to put it in a larger packing crate, lifting the lid idly to see what was in it.

Photos. Neatly stacked from front to back with little tabs every so often indicating the year. They went clear back to the year of her birth and he couldn't resist pulling one out and sneaking a peek.

There she was, a chubby-cheeked infant sitting in an apple basket, eyes crinkled in happy laughter. She'd been a damned cute baby. Is that what their children would look like?

Another picture showed her in the arms of a smiling woman who had to be her mother. The resemblance was astonishing. Her mother had had the same wealth of hair that Allison possessed, the same sweet smile and pretty eyes. She looked carefree and alluring, and he decided that if Allison ever let herself relax enough, she'd look just like that. Flipping the picture over, he read the note written in a sloping feminine hand: Nesta with Allison, 1 year old.

Another picture showed her mother with a handsome

cowboy in a light-colored hat, looking up at him with adoration in her eyes. The man looked into the camera with a confident smile, one arm slung loosely around the woman who hugged his waist, the other thumb hooked into his jeans pocket in a cocky pose. Something about the photo bothered Kane, though he couldn't quite figure it out. The guy looked as if he came with an attitude, and he wondered if the cowboy was Allison's father. He checked, but there was nothing written on the back of that one.

Others showed Allison as she grew older. First day of school, the one where she proudly showed a new gap in her teeth. One with an enormous white dog. Picture after picture of a beautiful child growing into a pretty young woman. Then the candid shots stopped abruptly. From the time she entered her teens, there were next to no pictures in the files, only the standard school shots and several yellowed newspaper clippings, evidence that she'd been on the honor roll at her high school.

Even then she'd worn her hair pulled tightly back. She stood in the second or third row, half-obscured by other students in most of the clippings. While other kids were looking straight into the camera with satisfied smiles, Allison's head was bent and she appeared to be looking at the ground. Making herself invisible. What was he missing? She'd told him her parents had divorced when she was twelve, and he realized the photos stopped right around the same time.

What exactly had happened between her parents that had changed her from a happy, grinning little girl into this serious, self-effacing adult?

He was so absorbed in the pictures that he never heard her come into the room until she said, "Wow. You've gotten a lot done…"

The sentence trailed away as she saw what he was looking at, and she made an effort to smile. "Found my checkered past, did you?" But the smile didn't reach her eyes and her voice was strained. She hurried over and began to shove photos randomly back into the box.

"Are these your parents?" He held up the photo of the man and woman he'd seen earlier.

"Yes." She didn't embellish it, didn't even look at the picture.

"We have something in common, then," he told her. "My father was a cowboy, too. Although he was a fancy rodeo man."

"My father, Micah, was a hand on a large ranch near Abilene, where I grew up." She put the lid on the box.

So she'd grown up near Abilene. It was more than he'd known before.

"Where is your father now?" he asked, eyes narrowing as he saw the way her hands were shaking.

She shrugged, not looking up at him. "He passed away eight months ago."

Eight months ago. And her mother had died a few years ago…probably during the time he'd known her. And yet she'd never said a word about losing either one of them. He was even more determined to learn more about her past.

He took the box from her and replaced the lid, then matter-of-factly placed it with some of the other things he'd packed, trying to sound casual. "Didn't you tell me they split up when you were about twelve?"

"I—yes, about twelve. It was a long time ago." Her voice was trembling now and he wanted to grab her and cuddle her against him until the stiffness left her body and she let herself cry, but he sensed she'd reject such comfort right now.

"That must have been tough," he said quietly. This was the key, he thought. The key that would unlock the puzzle of his too-quiet, too-cautious, too-careful Allison. But he didn't want to upset her so badly that she backed away from him. From the skittish way she was acting, she might even cancel their marriage if he pushed her too hard. He didn't know why he was so sure that her parents' divorce had made her into the woman she'd become, but he was. And he fully intended to learn why.

But not today. Quickly, he sealed the packing crate and lifted it onto the stack of boxes already waiting by the front door.

Allison had been standing with her back to him. He walked over and put his arms around her, dropping his head to nuzzle at her neck. "Are you ready to take some of this stuff over to your new home?" He'd intended the caress to be comforting, but when she immediately sighed and let herself relax against him, the familiar sexual interest tugged at his senses.

She tilted her head, giving him better access to her soft flesh and he slipped his palms up to cover her breasts, enjoying the shuddering breath she took as he plucked at the rising buds of her nipples beneath the knit shirt she wore. "I—suppose so," she said.

He waited for her to stop him, to tell him they had work to do, but when she pressed her tight little backside against him and her hands clasped his forearms, he groaned and slid one hand down her body, dragging up the skirt she wore by handfuls until he could feel her satiny belly beneath his hand. He plunged his hand under the edge of her lacy panties and boldly cupped her, finding to his delight that she was hot and wet for him already. His hips were grinding against her buttocks and he tugged until she came down with him to the carpet, spreading her legs for him as he fumbled to free himself from his pants and get the condom he'd finally gotten smart enough to put in his wallet.

When he entered her, her back arched and she made the little purring sound in her throat that he was beginning to recognize. Then they were moving together, sweet explosive passion flaring higher and higher.

It wasn't until much later that he remembered that he wasn't going to think about sex anymore that day.

Four

The next days passed quickly. Once Kane had made his mother understand that they wanted a small, intimate *fast* ceremony, Allison was amazed—and a little appalled—at how quickly things came together. A date was set for a Sunday afternoon just a little more than a week away.

Over several lunches that Kane insisted on attending, Miranda consulted Allison about her tastes and ideas.

"But honestly," Allison said several times, "whatever you think is best will be fine."

"It's your wedding, dear," Miranda said. "I want you to be happy and comfortable with it."

"Besides," said Kane, "If you tell her to do whatever she thinks is best, we're liable to wind up with orchestras and ice sculptures."

He'd intended to make her smile and she did. But she'd meant what she'd said about Miranda's planning. Marrying Kane would make her so happy that the ceremony and frills would be completely irrelevant. The only thing that would have thrown her was a crowd, and Kane had made it more than clear to his mother that the wedding was to be a private ceremony with only a few family attending.

Still, she was both thrilled and amazed when Miranda announced that she'd managed to reserve The Little Church of La Villita for the wedding. Actually, Allison suspected Miranda had bribed someone. Being married at La Villita was one of the few dreams that she'd actually dared to mention, more as a passing jest, really, and yet it was coming true. The ceremony would be held downtown near the river in the little church in the old historic district, something of which many San Antonio brides dreamed but few ever saw fulfilled.

She finished moving her things into Kane's home, and they hired movers to transport her furniture, most of which they intended to use until they got around to serious decorating efforts. The furniture had been her mother's and though it wasn't new, it was pretty and well cared for and wouldn't look out of place.

She worked another four-day week and was shocked when the other nurses and staff threw her a bridal shower on her last day of work before the wedding. Although Kane hadn't been invited to the all-girls event, he walked into the lounge as cake was being passed around.

"Hey," he said as someone cut him a hefty slice of cake. "My timing's great."

"Lordy, girl," said the respiratory specialist sitting on Allison's left side. The woman fanned herself as Kane smiled at one of the nurses. "If you need help handling all that man, feel free to give me a call."

Allison had to laugh. "I'll keep it in mind," she said dryly.

"Look, Dr. Fortune," called one of the licensed practical

nurses, the liveliest girl on the floor. She held up a sheer black chemise with dangling garters and lacy matching stockings. "We got *you* a gift, too!"

Kane grinned, turning to spear Allison with an intimate gaze. "And it'll be a pleasure unwrapping it."

There was a small, loaded silence. Allison could feel the heat of embarrassment turning her face the color of a vivid sundown. Someone murmured, "My, oh my, oh *my!* Where was he when *I* was husband-hunting?" and the moment passed in a round of laughter.

But she *hadn't* been husband-hunting, she thought to herself as the gathering ended and she closed her locker a quarter of an hour later. This all seemed like a fantastic dream...and she lived in fear that she was going to wake up.

Before Allison knew it, the eve of her wedding day arrived. They had planned no rehearsal since the ceremony was to be so small, with only Kane's mother, his uncle Ryan and his wife, and Kane's sister with her husband and daughter as witnesses, but Miranda insisted on giving them a small dinner party the night before the wedding. The older woman had encouraged Allison to invite her friends to the wedding, but Allison had gently declined. She couldn't invite a select few from the hospital staff without offending others. And there was no one else. After her parents' divorce, she'd become so close to her mother that there hadn't been any room, or any need, for intimate girlfriends. Her solitary nature had been fully formed by the time Nesta had died, and she'd found it easier to simply keep a small distance from those around her.

In addition to Kane's sister and brother-in-law, whom she'd met over dinner at Miranda's last week, his uncle Ryan and Ryan's wife, Lily, had been invited to the dinner.

Allison felt sick with nerves at the thought of meeting more members of the Fortune clan, especially Ryan Fortune, the well-known patriarch of the family. If Miranda thought there was something amiss in her son's choice of a bride, she certainly had hidden it well. She'd been nothing but wonderful to Allison in the past few days, so wonderful that Allison felt guilty and miserable for deceiving her.

Miranda clearly thought that her son was in love with Allison and she with him. Allison suspected that her feelings were blatantly transparent to Kane's mother's discerning eye, but she wondered why Miranda didn't more clearly see that love wasn't a part of what Kane felt for her.

He'd been acting oddly since the day he'd begun to move her into his home, occasionally appearing distant and distracted. She wanted to tell herself it was his work, but she was too honest to lie to herself. She was sure that Kane was regretting this whole mess. She wished he'd been willing to wait until they'd found out whether or not she was pregnant, but he was inflexible on the matter and loving him as she did, she simply couldn't bring herself to argue too vehemently. She wanted to be with Kane, wanted to marry him so badly that she didn't dare destroy the only chance she was ever likely to have to become his wife. He might not love her, but right now he wanted her and she could be content with that.

On the evening of the dinner, Kane called near four and told her he'd be delayed and would have to meet her there. A woman in pre-term labor was about to undergo a Caesarian section and they expected complications with the newborn. Consequently, Allison drove herself to Miranda Fortune's home with butterflies the size of crows flapping around in her stomach.

Kane's sport utility vehicle was nowhere in sight when she pulled in and parked and she sighed, forcing herself to collect her evening bag and slide out of the car. There were two other cars already parked around the circle, a low, sleek dark blue Ferrari and a gold Lexus which she knew belonged to Kane's sister. *Let the ordeal begin,* she thought morosely. Just then, Miranda came fluttering out of the house. In a floor-length chiffon layered tunic over slim pants, she resembled an exotic bird as she hurried toward Allison with her hands outstretched.

"Hello, dear," she said. "Kane called and told me he was going to be late and I didn't want you to have to walk in alone."

Allison felt a surge of tremendous affection for her almost-mother-in-law. "Thank you," she said. "I have to confess I'm a little nervous."

"There's no need. Really." Miranda linked an arm through hers and they moved toward the house. "You look lovely."

Allison smoothed a hand down over the vibrant aqua silk jacket covering a slim cocktail dress in the same shade. Kane had brought it home two days before, and asked her to wear it tonight. She'd found out he'd checked her closet for her clothing sizes and the dress fit like a dream. "Kane picked it out. I don't normally wear such bright colors."

"But it's stunning on you. You should wear this shade more often." Miranda opened the door and ushered Allison into the large foyer but instead of turning right into the small parlor where they usually visited, she took her to the left to the ivory-and-cream formal living room with its marble fireplace, handsome Oriental rugs in muted shades, and elegant chairs covered in watered silk moiré.

A tall dark-haired man in a linen suit stood near the fireplace. He was talking to Wyatt Grayhawk, Kane's brother-in-law, who had already slung his jacket over one shoulder. On a settee nearby, a dark, sophisticated older woman with her hair in a twist similar to Allison's sat talking to Gabrielle.

Everyone turned to look when Miranda and Allison entered, and the older man's gaze caught and held Allison's. For a moment she was staggered by his resemblance to Kane. Despite the darker hair and equally dark brown eyes, he possessed the same striking arrangement of features which made women long to catch Kane's attention.

"Allison's here," Miranda announced to the room at large. She escorted Allison across the room to the men, turning first to the older man. "This is my brother Ryan Fortune, and you've already met Wyatt." she said. "Ryan, this is Kane's fiancée, Allison Preston."

Wyatt nodded, a smile touching the corners of his usual reserved expression. Ryan Fortune smiled, extending a hand, and his dark eyes were warm. "It's good to meet you, Allison. Miranda has been singing your praises for a week now and I see she wasn't exaggerating."

She smiled, feeling utterly tongue-tied. This handsome man, along with his sister Miranda and his brother Cameron's children, was heir to one of the largest fortunes in Texas. The Fortunes were Texas's answer to the Kennedys of Massachusetts or the Windsors of England. She'd read about these people, seen snippets of their lives on television, almost all her life. She still felt as if she'd stepped into a fairy tale.

Miranda tugged Allison away from the men to where Gabrielle sat with Ryan's wife. "Lily, this is Allison."

Both women rose and Lily stepped forward to press a smooth cheek to hers. "Welcome to the family, dear," she said, her striking dark eyes twinkling.

"Thank you."

"Miranda tells us Kane's been delayed." Lily's gaze was steady. "I imagine that's a given in a doctor's life."

Allison smiled. "That *is* a doctor's life."

Just then, the sound of a car door closing intruded on the moment.

"That must be him," Allison said. "Excuse me." She hurried across the room, reaching the doorway just as the front door opened and Kane entered. He was still knotting his tie and his eyes looked tired. Then he glanced up.

He stopped dead when he saw her, and his eyes ran down over her dress. "You look…every bit as great as I imagined you would in that," he said in a deep, low voice. "But there's one thing wrong."

"What?" The pleasure she'd felt at his compliment faded instantly and consternation replaced it.

He crossed the foyer in three strides. "This," he said, and he reached up and began to pull the pins from her hair.

"Kane! Stop that!" She grabbed his wrists but he was far stronger than she and he continued to work until her hair fell down from the tidy twist she'd created.

As her hair came cascading around them, Kane speared his fingers into it, cradling her skull and pulling her up on tiptoe against him. "There," he said. "That's better."

His mouth sought hers as his fingers cupped her jaw, invading with the desire he seemed to have for her all the time, and she forgot everything but the man who held her in his arms. She loved him so very much she ached with it and her hands slipped around his waist as she leaned into him. He deepened the kiss, playing with her tongue and she tasted urgency in it, but finally he drew away, looking down at her with brilliant, narrowed eyes. "This will have to keep until later," he said in an undertone before he turned her around.

And it wasn't until she'd taken a step back toward the drawing room that she realized Miranda, Ryan, Lily, Gabrielle and Wyatt were all crowded in the doorway, watching them with frank, amused eyes.

Wyatt's eyes were on the rippling curtain of Allison's hair flowing around her. "That's…remarkable," he said to no one in particular. His wife nudged him sharply in the ribs with her elbow.

"Quit drooling, dear," she said, and Ryan began to chuckle aloud as Allison blushed furiously.

Kane looked at his assembled family. Over Allison's head, he saw his sister exchange a satisfied wink with her husband, and he eyed her narrowly until she looked his way again. When she saw his face, Gabrielle burst out laughing. "Why, hello, Kane! Now that you're finished greeting Allison maybe you have time to spare for the rest of your family?"

Kane snarled, but it was a teasing sound as he slid an arm around Allison's waist and took her to his sister's side. "Hello, brat. Better be nice or I'll disinvite you to the wedding tomorrow."

"If you don't let me come, you won't get to see Patience," she said smugly, referring to Kane's niece, Wyatt and Gabrielle's young daughter.

Gabrielle's words were lost on Kane as he simply stared at Allison, who was laughing at the exchange. Had he ever seen her smile like that? She was beautiful when she forgot to hold all her shining personality inside. God, he couldn't wait to get this dinner over with. Couldn't wait to get her home. But even more, he couldn't wait until after tomorrow, when she was legally his and nothing could take her away from him.

As he realized what he was thinking, he automatically backed away from her a pace. He wasn't going to let himself need Allison, or anyone, so badly that he couldn't live without her. He had a life, a perfectly acceptable life with a wonderful family whom he was still discovering and getting to know even after six years. But he'd lived without them, without anyone but his mother and sister, for most of his life and he wasn't about to let himself become dependent on anyone. He'd refused to let the Fortunes take him over, make him a part of what he privately thought of as "the Empire." He didn't need anyone and life would be simpler if he kept it that way.

When you kept it simple, you didn't get hurt.

"What's wrong?" Allison had approached him and was stroking the back of his hand. "Did that delivery go very badly this evening?"

"No, it was all right." He could feel the tension and ill humor draining out of him at the look of gentle concern in her eyes and the touch of her fingers on him. She was the most soothing woman he'd ever known.

Forcing himself to pull away from her magical touch was difficult. And because it was, his ill humor returned full force. After the wedding he'd have to explain to her that he needed space.

Allison cast him a puzzled glance, but she didn't try to touch him again and he could almost feel her withdrawing. Perversely, her reaction annoyed him, and he reached out and took her hand in his, bending her fingers to twine with his. She didn't look up at him, but he felt her hand soften and clutch his almost desperately. What the hell. He could worry about regaining his space later. He'd had one incredibly lousy day and just touching her made it recede in his mind. What was so wrong with that?

His mother called them all in to dinner then and the group headed for the dining room. His mother's face was shining as he looked at her. Miranda glanced down at his hand clasping Allison's and the way her fingers were stroking over his knuckles, and her smile deepened. "I'd have gone out and found her years ago if I'd known anyone could have such an effect on you," she told him.

He frowned automatically, not liking the implication, but before he could disclaim Allison's supposed effect on him, Miranda was handing around glasses of champagne in tall fluted glasses. "Would you offer the toast, Ryan?"

Over the meal, Allison slowly relaxed and his family appeared to be enchanted with her. At one end of the table, his mother talked animatedly to Lily about last-minute wedding plans, her hands moving in counterpoint to her rapid-fire words. His tension returned as he watched her, noting the almost manic bubbliness in her manner.

Miranda had thrown herself into planning the wedding with all her considerable energies. He was aware that his mother needed to occupy her mind right now. The strain of waiting for her ex-husband's next move was beginning to show on her lovely face; her blue eyes were haunted. Unbidden, the reason for this wedding skated into his mind. If Allison were pregnant, it would take his mother's mind off her problems.

The merest suggestion of a quiver of excitement ran through him. What would it be like to hold his own child in his arms? To know that there was someone in the world who needed and depended on him as no one else ever had? He'd never known that, never had a father to talk to. He'd taken care of his mother and sister for so long that he couldn't remember what it was like to be the one leaning on another. Besides, he thought, at this stage of his life, it wasn't necessary anymore. But if Allison was pregnant and they soon had a child of their own, he made a silent vow: his child would never, *never* fall asleep at night wondering what kind of man could walk away from his family.

And if Allison were pregnant, she wouldn't leave him.

It hadn't escaped him that she'd been less than enthusiastic about marrying him, had expressed doubts on several occasions since. But he knew her well enough to know that if she bore his child, she'd never walk away.

It wasn't that he *needed* her, he reminded himself, putting up a hand to stroke down the length of her hair where it fell over the back of her chair. It was just that he'd come to like the cozy way his home felt when she was in it. He liked the way she could make his bad days fade away with her soothing touch and gentle conversation. He liked the way she lifted her face for his kiss, the way her body softened against his in bed, the little purring noises she made when he entered her.

She turned her head and smiled at him then, her hand slipping over to squeeze his thigh beneath the table, and he tugged on her tresses.

"Don't start anything you're not prepared to finish." He leaned over and growled the words into her ear, pausing to kiss the tender flesh as he did so.

Her cheeks were a brilliant shade of pink and her eyes danced as she brought a hand to his chest and held him away from her. "I'm not starting anything here. You've already embarrassed me enough in front of your family!"

He found himself grinning like an idiot, but as he glanced across the table and caught his sister's speculative expression, he schooled his features into nonchalance. Of course he didn't *need* Allison. There was nothing wrong, though, with liking the way she enhanced his life.

Dinner was a success, as far as he could tell. His sister, mother and Aunt Lily pulled Allison into their conversation as if she'd always been a member of the family. They plied her with questions about her work and the hospital, and he could see her coming out of her shell, blooming beneath the attention, sharing the work that he knew she loved and in the process, sharing her own unique sweetness. Over dessert, he caught Wyatt eyeing her hair across the table again, and he sent him a razor-sharp smile. "Ogle your own wife, sheriff. This one's mine."

Wyatt only smiled as Ryan chuckled. "I might adore my wife but I'm not blind." He raised one eyebrow. "You, on the other hand, might be. Did I hear you say you've known her for four years?"

"Not everyone moves as fast as you and Gabrielle," Ryan said. "It took me far too long to figure out that Lily was what my life was missing."

But as the conversation moved on, Kane sat silently. He *had* known her for a long time before he'd decided to marry her. And he'd only done that because he'd taken her virginity during one of the darkest moments in his life. But now, as he thought about it, he realized that a part of him had come to value Allison a long time ago.

He'd told himself it was a casual work friendship, but the truth was he'd sought her out more and more often, drawn to her quiet, soothing presence. He'd sensed even then that she would be there for him, hadn't he? And he'd taken advantage of it, monopolizing her and keeping her from developing other friendships, other relationships.

A vivid memory of a conversation with another doctor over a year ago sprang into his head, a conversation that he'd have sworn he'd forgotten until moments ago. He'd been in the cafeteria with Allison when another resident had joined them at the small table where they were sharing coffee and donuts. Allison had included the man with her usual gentle graciousness and the other guy, a nonstop comic, had had her in stitches within minutes.

When she'd glanced at her watch and risen, the other doctor had started to accompany her from the room but

Kane had cut him off with a curt word and walked with her back to the N.I.C.U. Hours later, he'd run into the guy.

"Hey, Fortune," the resident had said. "Do you go out with Allison Preston?"

Kane had merely stared at the other man.

"Because if you don't," the guy plowed on, "I'm going to ask her to a movie or something."

Kane had continued to stare at the doctor as impotent fury rose in his system. She wasn't his, he reminded himself. They were just friends. Even so, the guy standing in front of him wasn't nearly good enough for her. He was pleasant enough, but he had a reputation for loving and leaving women, and the string of broken hearts he'd left through the hospital was proof enough for Kane. Allison deserved someone who would really treat her as if she were the most important thing in his life. Finally, unable to combat the instinct rushing through him, he'd said, "Stay away from Allison."

There had been enough of a snarl in his tone to make the other man raise his eyebrows and shrug his shoulders. "Hey, man, didn't mean to step on your toes," he'd said.

He *hadn't* stepped on Kane's toes, Kane told himself. It was just that he hadn't wanted to see Allison taken in by someone who didn't recognize what a treasure she was.

Allison's wedding day dawned clear and sunny and by midmorning it was already unseasonably warm for a late January day at seventy-six degrees. A perfect day for a wedding.

Shortly before the eleven o'clock marriage service was set to begin, they took the interstate downtown to the River Walk and the historic La Villita district bounded by King Phillip Walk, Villita Street and Alamo Street. The Little Church was tucked in between a jewelry shop and an art gallery, with yet another gallery of small shops flanking the courtyard behind it.

Miranda, Ryan and Lily were already at the church when they arrived, and Miranda and Lily joined Allison on the wide tiled pavement outside while Ryan took Kane up the steps through the narrow arched doorway. The stained-glass depiction of a cross above the altar glowed in rich jewel-like hues through the huge glass panes in the heavy doors.

"Here you are, dear." Lily handed her a trailing bouquet of stargazer lilies and palest pink roses nestled in ivy and ferns. She pinned a matching corsage on Miranda and went off in search of the men with rose boutonnieres in her hand.

"You look so lovely." Miranda's eyes filled with tears.

"It's the dress." Allison smoothed a hand over the simple, tea-length white silk. "I would never have found anything so beautiful without your help." Miranda had taken her shopping for a wedding dress, calmly ignoring her protests that a suit would do. Kane had told her he wanted Allison in white, she'd said, and that was the end of that.

"It's not the dress." Miranda smiled. "Though it *is* a gorgeous garment. It's you, dear. You glow." She glanced toward the front of the church, where Kane and Ryan were conferring with Lily and the minister before the simple wooden altar. Set on its plain surface were stunning sprays of pink and white gladiolus with more roses and lilies, while the seven tapers of the candelabra on each side were interlaced with ivy, roses and babies' breath. The same theme was echoed in the small wooden railings that flanked each side of the altar. "Isn't the church gorgeous?"

"It is." Her voice was reverent. "I still can't believe we're getting married here." She laughed self-consciously. "I still can't believe we're getting married, *period.*"

"You are," said Miranda positively. "And not soon enough for me. Kane can't afford to let you get away."

Her eyes softened. "I always worried so about him. The few of his dates I met were shallow and self-centered. They were too busy checking out their images in mirrors to really care about Kane. I was beginning to fear he chose that kind of woman on purpose. My son is a very solitary man, and a woman like that wouldn't threaten his solitude." She paused. "But you...you couldn't be more different. Kane's more open, happier than I've ever seen him. I thank you for loving him."

"I've loved him since the first time I met him." She smiled tremulously. She wished his mother's words were true, but she certainly hadn't seen any signs that she made Kane particularly happy, except in a purely physical context. In fact, the opposite was true. He seemed moodier and more introspective now than he had before. "But I never imagined he'd notice me."

"Well, I thank heaven he did!"

She might have commented further, but there was no point in bursting his mother's bubble.

Miranda turned away from her then, reaching for a dry-cleaning bag and extracting a long swath of Spanish lace. "Here's the veil I promised you." She held up the delicate fabric. "It belonged to Rosita Perez, the housekeeper who practically raised me as well as both my brothers' children. A number of Fortune and Perez brides have worn it and it will mean a lot to Ryan."

"It's so gorgeous." Allison stood motionless while Miranda pinned the veil in place and arranged it over her long, unbound hair. "Thank you for sharing it with me."

"It's *my* pleasure. I never wore it," Miranda said wistfully.

"There's still time," Allison said. "You never know. Your Prince Charming might be standing right around the next corner."

But Miranda didn't smile. "I met my Prince Charming years ago and I blew it. Since then, I've made a career out of kissing frogs. If I can just get through the rest of my life without screwing it up any more than I already have, I'll be content."

"Content isn't the same as happy; I think you should try for happy." Allison put an arm around Miranda's shoulder, rubbing her upper arm and tactfully changing the subject. "I want to thank you for everything you did to make today special. The only thing that could make it better would be to have my own mother with us."

Miranda returned the hug, careful not to squash the bouquet. "I wish she could be, too, dear. I'm sure she's watching you, though." Her voice wavered and both women sniffed. "Kane will kill me if I make you cry," she said, chuckling.

"All right. I think we're ready!" Lily came rustling back the aisle, beaming. "Gabrielle and Wyatt just arrived." She stopped a few feet from Allison. "Oh, honey, you look so lovely. Your hair and that veil…and your dress…" Her dark eyes sparkled. "Kane's going to be bowled over when he sees you!" She stepped forward and enveloped Allison in a gentle hug, kissing her cheek. "Good luck, dear."

Ryan strode back across the dark red carpet, beaming. "All right, Allison. Are you ready? Kane says we're supposed to get this show on the road." He paused, a gleam of masculine appreciation in his eye. "You look fetching." Then he offered his arm to his sister. "Come on, Miranda. Time for a front-row seat."

He was back in a moment, offering his arm to Allison.

"Thank you for escorting me," she said, a little awed. How was it possible that Ryan Fortune was walking her up the aisle at her wedding? Then a pang of sorrow and regret struck her. Even if he'd lived, her father probably wouldn't have been here, performing this traditional task. She hadn't been ready to forgive him eight months ago. No, she'd still be wallowing in righteous anger and disdain, taking a mean pleasure in denying him the chance to walk her down the aisle. The thought brought the hovering tears back again and she tilted her face to the ceiling, fiercely blinking them away.

"It's my pleasure, dear," Ryan assured her, recalling her from the momentary introspection. "I thought my chance to do this had ended when Vanessa, Victoria and Gabrielle were married. It's truly my pleasure."

He turned and nodded through the vestibule doors at the organist who'd been quietly providing background music. As the swells of the Lohengrin wedding march began, he leaned over and lightly kissed Allison's forehead. "Welcome to the family."

The ceremony was brief and conventional, but thanks to Miranda, it was perfectly done. As she walked steadily up the aisle on Ryan's arm, between pews of antique, gleaming carved wood, she kept her focus on Kane. His face was sober, but a gleam of appreciation in his eyes reassured her and told her that he found her attire pleasing. A strong surge of happiness warmed her as he took her hand from Ryan, who returned to stand between Miranda and Lily; Gabrielle and Wyatt stood across the aisle with Patience.

Since she had no family present, they'd dispensed with the giving away of the bride, and before she knew it, she was repeating her vows to Kane in a quiet, steady voice. Then he said his, his gaze holding hers. She was dimly aware of Miranda crying quietly in the background as her heart gathered each word and tucked it away to be treasured forever. They exchanged the rings they'd bought and after a brief blessing, she was pronounced Mrs. Kane Fortune to the sound of her husband's family's clapping.

After the ceremony, Miranda guided them around the low stone wall and the iron fence around the back to the stone fountain in the courtyard, where the photographer who'd snapped discreet pictures throughout the ceremony posed them on the wide, shallow steps of the fountain for more formal portraits. As the man snapped shot after shot, Allison wondered if the love she felt for the tall, dark man beside her would show in her face when the photos were developed.

Five

———

The wedding luncheon his mother had arranged at a nearby hotel seemed to take forever. Kane could hardly contain his impatience though he knew the meal would please his mother. He just wanted all this to be over, wanted to get into a normal routine with his wife.

His wife. He'd never expected to like the sound of the words so much. As the waiter came around to offer coffee to everyone at the table, he decided he'd had enough wedding. Time for the good part.

He stood, holding out his hand for Allison. She stood and placed her hand in his, a mildly puzzled expression on her lovely face.

"We have to leave now," he informed her.

"Oh." She looked slightly disquieted. "But our guests—"

"Can entertain themselves," he informed her. "We have a honeymoon suite awaiting."

"A honeymoon suite!" She looked stunned. Then her face lit up with a smile of such spontaneous beauty she looked incandescent. "But you said we didn't have time for a honeymoon."

He grinned, glad he'd been able to surprise her. "Well, we don't. But I thought we should do something special on our wedding night. I booked a suite at La Mansion del Rio for the night."

"La Mansion!" Allison's face reflected her shock. "Oh, Kane!"

La Mansion was one of the River Walk's finest hotels, a former boys' college that boasted some of the most beautiful views of the river. It was arguably one of San Antonio's most exclusive hotels. Kane had never had occasion to stay there, but he'd heard that despite its unprepossessing exterior it was extraordinarily beautiful inside. He couldn't think of a better place for their wedding night and from the way she threw her arms around his neck and kissed him while his family laughed and clapped, he decided he'd pleased his bride as well.

"Are you sure?" she asked him. "I know you have rounds."

"I'm sure," he said, lightly holding her by the waist. "I called Dr. Ankra and she agreed to take my rounds today if I'll cover her tomorrow night. In fact, she was delighted to help out and asked me to give you her congratulations."

"All right. We'll have to go home first so I can pack—"

"That's all taken care of." he told her. "I gave the housekeeper a list this morning while we were downtown at the wedding. The bag is in the trunk of my car." He smiled down into her eyes, feeling her soft curves beneath his hands, suddenly impatient to be alone with her. "Come on, wife. Our honeymoon awaits."

* * *

The drive went quickly. Kane turned onto College Street and they checked in. The hotel staff was smiling and helpful as they were taken to their suite and he realized that with Allison still wearing her wedding dress, their new status was readily apparent.

The one-bedroom suite was charming, done in Spanish colonial style. The bellman brought up their single suitcase and then they were alone together. Dr. and Mrs. Kane Fortune. He liked the sound of it. He liked the thought of it, of picturing Allison coupled with him forever.

She'd moved through the suite to the pretty balcony that overlooked the river while he'd conferred with the bellman and he joined her there, leaning on the railing and looking out at the beautifully landscaped grounds below them.

"Thank you," she said.

"You're welcome." Just standing close to her, watching the gentle rise and fall of her breasts as she breathed, feeling the warmth she radiated, made him want her. He straightened and put a hand on her arm, drawing her back into the room and sliding his arms around her. "What do I have to do to get you out of this dress?" he asked as he shut the balcony door.

She smiled. "It's easy. There's a zipper in the back. Your mother wanted to have it replaced with a million little buttons—it was one of the few things I actually had to tell her I didn't want to do."

He was already drawing down the zipper, and the dress fell into a white puddle at her feet. As he lifted her free of the fabric, his mouth fell open. "Where did you get *that?*"

She was wearing a fire-engine red bustier that cupped her full breasts and plumped them into tempting mounds of alabaster flesh that barely concealed soft pink nipples. The lace faithfully followed the curve of her waist and flared out again, stopping at her hips to reveal a tiny triangle of red panties. Garter straps hung from the bustier were attached to sheer, pearly silk stockings. She was still wearing her white strappy heels. He couldn't resist dropping to his knees before her and kissing the soft skin of her upper thigh that was revealed above the stocking.

"Your sister gave it to me last night." She put her hands on his head, running them gently through his hair. "She made me promise to wear it today."

"Remind me to thank her. It's a good thing I didn't know you had this on under that dress," he said, dragging his mouth over silk and flesh, "or we might not have made it to the altar."

A loud knock at the door made her jump. "Heavens! Who could that be?"

Kane rose to his feet with a sigh. "Don't move. Not an inch." He walked to the door, withdrawing a tip from his pocket. He signed the tab and dismissed the waiter, then wheeled the small cart into the room himself.

"Champagne and canapés," he said to Allison. "I thought we should start this marriage off right."

"This is—it's very thoughtful." Her eyes were huge and they looked suspiciously shiny and he knew a moment's guilt. She hadn't had much reason to expect romance from him in the weeks since they'd decided to marry.

"I wanted it to be special for you." She hadn't moved yet, and he crossed to her, taking her hand and leading her to the tray.

She looked down at herself. "Kane! I can't walk around like this!" Her cheeks were bright red.

"Why not? There's no one but me to see you." He grinned as he caught the back view in the big mirror on the wall and realized the tiny panties were a thong. "And quite a sight you are." He slid a hand around her back then smoothed it down across the firm, naked swell of her bottom. Then he took his palm away with a rueful chuckle. "Maybe the champagne wasn't such a great idea. I'm not sure I can keep my hands off you long enough to open it."

"It was a wonderful idea," she whispered. "I truly didn't expect you to take time away from work, but I'm glad you did."

Her gratitude made him feel uneasy and small. Why had he resisted the idea of a honeymoon so much? He'd told himself—and her—that he couldn't take a week away but the truth was he'd never taken a single vacation in his four years at County and he was long overdue for a break.

But Allison seemed to expect so little that she'd never even questioned his statement that he couldn't get away. He'd taken for granted the easy way she'd wound herself into the pattern of his days. She never demanded anything, never nagged. She was unfailingly supportive, warm and willing.

He felt guilty and ashamed, and he vowed to do better. He'd done so little to show her that he liked the way she'd changed his life. But he hoped the meal awaiting them would tell her. He'd left instructions with the concierge while he was checking their luggage.

Forcing himself to ignore the lush bounty of feminine treasure standing just inches away, he moved to the cart. He cut the foil on the bottle and opened the wire, then draped a napkin over the cork as he gently uncorked the champagne—a fairly light-bodied vintage that he'd thought would go well with the refreshments.

"You do that like an expert," she observed with a smile.

"I like wine," he said as he handed her a bubbling glass, "so I've learned a good bit about it."

"All I know about wine would fit right here." She indicated the tip of her smallest finger.

He chuckled. "Then it's a good thing you have me now."

Her smile faltered. "I still can't believe we're married."

"Believe it." He stepped to her side and slipped his arm around her, drawing her scantily clad body against his and closing his eyes in delight for a moment at the feel of her all along his length. Opening his eyes, he lifted his glass slightly. "I propose a toast."

She lifted hers in response, her eyes on his.

"To the joys of marriage." He touched her glass with his.

"To the joys of marriage," she repeated softly, and they each took a drink.

He could have let it go, but the toast had sounded hollow and impersonal to him, and he couldn't manage to step away from her. He set his glass against hers again, holding her eyes. "And to my beautiful wife and the many happy years we'll share."

Tears rose in her eyes almost instantly. "To many happy years," she whispered.

They each drank again, then he set his glass aside. He reached for hers and did the same, pulling her more snugly against him. "This is driving me wild," he growled. "I was going to take you down to the River Walk before our dinner reservations, but..."

"But..." She shifted her body against his once, then again. "We can always come down to the River Walk. We only have one night here." Her voice dropped. "Maybe we should reorder our priorities."

He chuckled deep in his throat. "I'll drink to that," he said as he lowered his head and took her mouth. She responded immediately with the sweet hot fire he'd learned to expect, nearly burning him alive as she slipped her arms up around his neck and ran her fingers through his hair, caressing his skull.

His pulse was pounding already, almost out of control, his body surging heavily against her through the constricting fabric of his pants. He tore his mouth from hers and tugged the bustier down, making a sound of approval low in his throat as he exposed her breasts. "Mine," he said, cupping one plump mound and lifting it free. "Mine." He bent so that he could take the small taut tip into his mouth and pressed it firmly against the roof of his mouth, suckling strongly.

She gave a short scream and wriggled against him, her hands clenching in his hair. Then her arms came down between them and she tore frantically at his clothing. First she opened his shirt, and small arrows of fire sizzled through him when her palms covered his flat nipples. He groaned when she freed him and took him between her small, warm palms. Then her hand moved lower, between his legs. She slipped her palm beneath him, cupping him and stroking gently with a single finger and he thought he was going to lose it right there. "Stop," he gasped, seizing her hand and dragging it away. He was hot and hard; her belly where he brushed it was soft and silky and he couldn't resist the urge to roll his hips heavily against her as he fumbled in his pocket for the protection he'd brought along.

She was smiling into his eyes as her hips accepted the press of his flesh. "Look," she said.

He glanced down and another surge of heavy lust roared through him. The tiny red panties tied at the hip; as he watched, her slender fingers tugged loose the tiny fastenings. The panties slipped away, to be discarded on the floor, leaving her clad only in the disheveled bustier, silky stockings and high heels.

He sucked in a breath. "If you're trying to drive me

insane, you're going about it right." His voice sounded like a stranger's, deep and rough. He set his hands at her hips and lifted her, bracing her back against the wall as she wrapped her silk-clad legs around him. The moist cove between her legs pressed against his length for a moment, then he moved back and shoved himself inside her, using her weight to slide himself deeply into her. At his back, he could feel the dig of a heel into his buttock; it was incredibly arousing. A mad wildfire tore through him, burning away restraint. He held her pinned against the wall as he began to thrust—long, powerful strokes that made her writhe and cry out each time he pressed forward again. "Look at us," he said hoarsely, watching himself penetrate her humid depths. She did as he directed, a long moan shuddering out of her at the erotic sight.

The sound of her arousal signaled the end of his control. He anchored her with his hands clasping the soft globes of her bottom and the wall supporting her weight as he increased the driving speed of his thrusts, hammering a frantic beat that lasted only moments before he stiffened and shattered as he spent himself. She convulsed around him at the very moment of his release, and he shivered in reaction when her soft flesh squeezed him repeatedly. His body sagged against her as the intense climax receded and he buried his head in her neck for long moments until finally he could breathe again. He raised his head, looking into her eyes as he set his mouth on hers and kissed her deeply.

Lifting his head again, he looked around them and began to laugh. "Oops. The bed's over there."

He felt her tighten around him as she chuckled, too. "Oh, well. We can try it out later."

"Later? What's wrong with now?"

"Now?" She sounded startled. "But I thought you'd need time..."

He thrust once, letting her know that their recent love-making had done little more than take the edge off, and her eyes fluttered closed. He freed himself and set her down long enough to step out of his pants. Then he retrieved fresh birth control before lifting her into his arms again.

Wryly, she smiled as she shook her head. "Mm-m-m."

He clasped his hands more firmly beneath her bottom and began to walk across the room toward the bed, and he shuddered, feeling the rise of a pulsing need beating through his veins again.

"On second thought," she said as they passed the wide mirrored desk. "The bed's awfully far away. Do you think you can make it?"

He turned, still holding her, so that his buttocks rested on the desk. He braced his legs wide apart, letting her weight sink fully over him again before he lifted her and began to move her up and down in an easy rhythm that made her eyes close again and her head fall back in pleasure.

"Oh, I can make it," he said. "But I can't make it to the bed. Not this time."

The rest of the day was perfect, as far as she was concerned. They had time for a short stroll along the River Walk before dinner. As they walked along the wide stone pathway, occasionally passing beneath the graceful trees that arched over the green currents of water, Kane held her hand, his thumb brushing absently over the ring he'd put on her finger. They didn't talk much, and she wondered if his body felt as tingly as hers did, as if each cell had been sensitized by their earlier lovemaking.

Dinner was at Boudro's on the River Walk, and he'd specifically requested a table right beside the river. There was a bottle of champagne chilling in a silver bucket and a large spray of white roses graced the table to which the maître d' led them. She could feel tears rising in her eyes, and she turned to him, lifting herself on tiptoe to kiss his newly-shaven jaw.

"Thank you," she said, "For making this so special."

"I wanted it to be special," he said. "This is the first day of our lives together. It should be memorable, something we can tell our children." He grinned. "God knows, we're going to have to censor what we tell them about how we first met!"

She made a face at him. "We worked together," she summarized. "And one day we just realized we wanted to get married."

"A little skimpy on details, isn't it?" Kane chuckled. "You'd better hope we have a son instead of a daughter. I can't imagine a girl being satisfied with a wimpy explanation like that."

Son...daughter. His handsome features blurred around the edges as she gazed at him across the table and her happiness faded slightly. She'd been feeling the heavy, bloated feeling that usually preceded her period for the past few days. She doubted that they were going to have to worry about an unplanned pregnancy, and though she should be pleased, she *wanted* Kane's baby so badly...

"What's wrong?" He reached around the lighted candle centerpiece and took her hands in his.

"Nothing." She managed a smile. "I was just thinking about how lovely the ceremony was."

He accepted her words at face value, thanking her for the way she'd let his mother help with the wedding, and then the waiter came to take their order.

Their loveplay continued during dinner. She slipped her foot out of her sandal and rubbed it lightly up his leg; he nearly jumped out of his chair. "Stop that," he muttered, trying his best to scowl at her. "Or the other diners are going to get a shock when I stand up."

She was giggling helplessly as she removed her foot.

"*If* I can stand up," he added.

When the meal ended, the same waiter brought out a single slice of lemon cake for them to share. She was touched. Kane had recently learned that lemon cake was one of her weaknesses. For a man who hadn't had time to take a honeymoon, he certainly had put a great deal of thought into making this one evening special for her.

Before they left the restaurant, he had the roses wrapped in paper and gave them to her.

But the evening wasn't over yet. He hailed one of the pretty boats that plied the river and helped her in, paying the guide so that he wouldn't pick up any additional passengers. Kane led her to the graceful bench along the very back and they sat beneath the lights of swaying paper lanterns spaced along the boat's canopy, letting the water rock them. Kane's arm encircled her and she sat with her head on his shoulder, more content than she'd ever imagined she could be.

No matter what happens in the future, she thought, *I'll always have this.*

His shoulder shifted beneath her then, and she looked up at him in enquiry.

In answer, he slipped his hand out of the pocket into which he'd reached and set a small, silver-wrapped box in her lap.

"What's this?" She touched the shiny ribbon with a tentative finger.

"A gift for my bride." His eyes were warmer than she'd ever seen them, and his palm caressed the ball of her shoulder.

"But I didn't get you anything!" She was dismayed. Beyond dismayed. She'd never expected this.

"Allison." He cradled her jaw, using his thumb to tilt up her face so she would meet his eyes. "You've changed my life in so many ways, all for the better. Don't you know you've given me more gifts already than I can count?"

She swallowed, touched to tears by his words.

"Now open your present." He picked up the box again and held it under her nose. "Aren't you the least little bit curious?"

She smiled ruefully. "You know me too well." Taking the box from him, she shook it gently near her ear, then slowly and carefully untied the ribbon and set it aside. She pried up the tape that closed one end of the package without tearing the paper and carefully smoothed back the wrapping.

"Don't tell me you're one of *those*." Kane sighed with exaggerated impatience. "I can't stand the suspense. Just open it."

"But I like to take my time." She patted his cheek. "Once it's open, all the suspense is over." Slowly, she lifted the lid on the small box. Inside was an item heavily swathed in tissue on a bed of dark blue velvet. She carefully pushed aside the tissue—

And there, sparkling in her palm, was a miniature crystal kitten, posed in a playful position with a ball of yarn crafted of gold whose strands were tangled around the tiny cat.

She drew in a shocked breath and promptly burst into tears.

"Wha—" Kane straightened and took the crystal figure from her, setting it carefully in its box before drawing her against his chest. "Don't you like it? I can return it?" His usually unflappable voice held a distinct note of panic.

"No, it's not that." She stifled a sob. "It's lovely."

"Then…what?" He combed his fingers through her hair and held her face away from his chest so that he could see her expression.

She sniffled, closing her eyes. "It's just that…you remembered my collection. This year was the first birthday in my whole life that I didn't receive a little cat. No matter where my father was or who he was married to at the time, he never forgot. Even though I never did anything more than write him a killingly polite thank-you note, he still remembered my birthday every single year." She sighed, stroking the tiny kitten with a gentle finger. "It's a beautiful, thoughtful gesture, Kane. And you'll never know how much it means to me. Thank you."

He kissed her forehead. "You're welcome. Just look at it this way: your father passed on the torch to your husband. Your crystal cats are a tradition carried on by the men in your life."

She almost sobbed aloud again, regret for the years she'd denied her father nearly choking her.

Apparently sensing her inner anguish, Kane pulled her close again, stroking her back with his large palms. "He knows, Allison. Even though he's not here, I'm sure he knows you care."

She nodded against his chest. "I hope so."

There was a long, comfortable silence between them as the boat glided along the serene water of the river. She replaced the gift in its box, and Kane tucked it into his pocket for safekeeping.

After a long time, she said, "I used to play with the cats when I was little. My mother always fussed at me when she caught me. I'm sure she was afraid I'd break one. But after my father left, she never even noticed when I got them out."

"Too busy trying to make ends meet?"

"No." Allison shook her head. "Daddy might not have been good about visiting but he was faithful about child support." She shrugged. "After he left, Mom stayed in bed all the time."

"*All* the time?"

She nodded, reliving the dull, deadened atmosphere of her childhood in those days. "She was in bed when I left for school, and still in bed when I got home at the end of the day. Sometimes she'd get up and fix dinner, but mostly she forgot. I realize now she was depressed, but back then, all I knew was my father did that to her. To me."

Kane stroked her hair. "Sounds pretty terrible."

She nodded quietly. "It was. Mom gradually got better, but she was never the same after that." She made an effort to shake off the dark mood, not wanting to spoil the perfect evening he'd planned, saying in a lighter tone, "I guess we both had deadbeat dads, didn't we?"

He murmured assent.

"But that was a long time ago. And look at us now." Smiling, she turned into his arms. "You've made me happier than you'll ever know."

"Good." His voice was thick as he sought her mouth, his kisses deep and possessive. "I want you to be happy."

They left the boat at the same point they'd picked it up and walked back along the river in silence, hands clasped. As they entered the lush grounds of their hotel, he stopped her and pulled her tightly against him, kissing her until her head swam and she clutched at his strong shoulders for support.

He lifted her into his arms, then, and carried her right into the hotel and up to their room, despite her embarrassed pleas to be set down. Finally, she simply gave up and buried her face in his shirt. She couldn't possibly look anyone in the eye.

Back in their room, he made love to her again and again, stroking and kissing her as if it were the first time.

Afterward, Allison slept through the night in her husband's arms and when he turned her on her back at dawn and entered her with slow, lazy strokes, she let the pleasure carry her along to an extended, pulsing climax that mirrored his. Then they showered together and ordered breakfast from the room-service menu before driving home to the northern suburbs.

They dropped by Miranda's home two days later to return the veil that Allison had had dry-cleaned. Kane came around to help Allison out of the Explorer and together they walked into the house. It gave her definite flutters in her stomach when she thought about the fact that she was a Fortune now.

Miranda came to greet them. "Would you like to stay for dinner? Don't feel you have to if you have other plans or you just want to be alone." She took Allison's hands. "I promise I won't be one of those needy, interfering mother-in-laws who can't let go of their little sons."

Allison laughed. "Somehow I can't make that image fit either you *or* Kane!"

They had an informal meal in the kitchen while his mother plied them for every detail about their honeymoon. Allison let Kane do most of the talking, knowing she would do nothing but blush if she thought about that magical twenty-four hours when Kane had seemed like a different man, a man who loved his new bride.

They were just finishing dinner when the stately chimes of the doorbell sounded. Miranda looked surprised. "I wasn't expecting anyone." She started to rise but Kane waved her back into her seat as he rose and laid his napkin aside. "Stay there, Mother. I'll get it."

He walked from the dining room into the foyer, striding across the imported Italian tiles and firmly swinging open the heavy doors. "Good evening. May I help you?"

There were two people standing on the stone of the entranceway, a man about his own height wearing a dressy ivory cowboy hat with a beaten silver band around the crown, and a woman in a too-tight, too-short pink dress who clung to his arm.

"I'm here to see Miranda Fortune." The man's voice was deep. It quivered slightly with nerves, and his gaze skittered to Kane's and away again. Was there something familiar about it? No, probably just a similarity to someone he'd talked with recently. As a doctor, Kane knew better than to make snap judgments, but something about this man made his hackles rise. There were always opportunists and hangers-on trying to ride on the Fortune coattails; he'd bet his last nickel this shifty cowboy was one of them.

"Ms. Fortune's not available at the moment," Kane said smoothly. "I suggest you call tomorrow for an appointment."

He started to shut the door, but the woman stepped forward and grabbed his arm. "Ms. Fortune's going to want to see us, mister."

"Hush up, Leeza." The man roughly pulled her back, but he put his booted foot in the door before Kane could close it. "Wouldja just get Miranda, mister? This won't take but a minute."

"Listen, cowboy," Kane said in a dangerously quiet voice. "You can leave quietly now or I can help you out. I can promise you won't like my assistance." He flexed his shoulders deliberately, holding his eye contact with the man.

"Kane?" Rapid footsteps on the tile alerted him just as his mother came up behind him. "Who is it?"

The cowboy's face creased into a more confident expression as he caught sight of Miranda. "Randi! I just got into town and I wanted to come by and say howdy." Then he turned an appraising eye on Kane, the skittishness apparently banished. "So you're Kane. I always wondered what kind of man you'd turned into."

"Lloyd." As his mother took a step backward, Kane instinctively put his arm around her, his mind reeling with shock.

The man with the weathered face and surprisingly charming smile standing in his mother's entry was his father. The man who'd never bothered to contact or see his family since Kane had been a year old.

Six

"Well, if this isn't just great." Lloyd Carter aimed a warm smile at his son. "You turned out just fine, boy."

"That's Dr. Fortune to you." Kane relaxed the fingers he'd curled into fists with a conscious effort.

"Doctor? You're a doctor? That's really something!" Then his tanned features clouded. "You changed your name to Fortune?"

Kane ignored the question. He held the pressure on the door, barely restraining himself from slamming it right on the cowboy's foot. "I can guess what you want."

"I bet you can." The woman in the pink dress spoke again. "Nice, smart fella like you—"

"This here's my wife, Leeza," Lloyd broke in. "We, uh, we—" He stopped, removed his hat and hauled out a large white handkerchief and mopped his shiny forehead with it. "We came to talk to your mother about a matter I brought up on the phone a few weeks ago."

"You mean your *blackmail* demands," said Kane between his teeth.

"This doesn't concern you, son," Lloyd said. "This is just a little private business between your mother 'n' me."

"*My* son and I have no secrets." Miranda tugged at Kane's sleeve, indicating that he should open the door. "Come into my study and tell us both your demands."

"Kane?" He turned as his mother led her unwanted guests into the room just off the foyer. Allison was hurrying toward him. "You've been gone a while. Is something wrong?"

"My father's here." He took her shoulders and turned her toward the dining room. "Trust me, you *don't* want to meet him. Mother and I will just be a few minutes." He let a breath of frustration hiss out between his teeth. "And if you hear screams, it'll be me choking that son-of-a-bitch."

Allison lifted her hands to his arms, her small thumbs rubbing across the veins and tendons of his inner wrists. Her eyes were wide and concerned. "Don't do anything rash," she said. Then she went back down the hall the way she'd come.

He turned on his heel and went into the study, where his mother had taken a seat behind her elegant lady's desk, leaving both strangers standing awkwardly in the middle of the room. Grimly amused at her tactics, he strode to her side, positioning himself just behind her.

"That little blonde your wife?" Lloyd settled himself in one of the wing chairs uninvited and his wife followed suit.

"Why do you need to know?" Kane shot him a furious look.

His father's shoulders seemed to slump. "No reason," he said. "I just wanted to know if you're happy."

"Your interest is a little late in coming."

Miranda cleared her throat. "Tell us what you want, Lloyd."

"Aw, for Pete's sake, you already know what we want!" Leeza Carter's strident voice grated nasally on his ear.

"I, ah, I have some information here—" Lloyd began.

"Don't even think about showing her that until you've got the money," his wife shrilled.

Lloyd's hands stopped fumbling with his pocket. An awkward silence fell.

"Lloyd, why are you doing this to me?" Miranda's lovely eyes were fastened on the man who'd once been her husband. "What did I ever do to you to deserve this?"

"Aw, Randi—"

"You've got plenty of money, lady. It's not like we're gonna break your bank." Leeza sat forward aggressively.

Miranda never even looked at the woman. "I'm speaking to Lloyd." Her voice was quiet but frosty and authoritative. With a huff, Leeza shoved herself back in the chair.

"Life's treated you better'n me, Randi." Lloyd's voice was subdued. "I've made some money in my time, but things are kind of pinching around the edges right now." His brows lowered and a hint of belligerence crept in. "I invested in a Phoenix cattle company a couple of years ago, looked like a real good deal, too. But then your brother got the contract we were looking at, and before I knew it, my stock was worth nothin'. Went belly-up. I had to go back on the circuit to make enough money to pay off my debt, and I *still* owe some."

"Yeah, and we got a right to make a living same as everybody else," his wife put in. "Fifty thousand is peanuts." She looked at Lloyd scornfully. "I told you we should have asked for a million!"

"Fifty thousand is all we need," Lloyd said, setting his jaw.

"Blackmail and extortion aren't a widely accepted means of making money." Miranda eyed her ex-husband. "If I pay you, how do I know you won't be back on my doorstep again next month, wanting another handout in exchange for silence?"

Lloyd raised his right hand. "I give you my word, that's how."

Kane didn't even try to hide the mocking chuckle that burst out. "And we all know how trustworthy *that* is. Look at how faithfully you upheld your marriage vows."

His father's neck flushed a dark red and the color slowly crept up. He turned to face Kane. "You don't know how it was, boy, so don't you be so righteous." He turned back to Miranda. "I wish I could do those years over again. I wasn't makin' enough to support you and the baby; you know I had to stay on the rodeo circuit. It isn't my fault it just never panned out like I thought it would."

"You don't owe them any apologies, Lloyd!" Leeza's voice was sharp. "Let's just get what we came for and get out of here."

Kane watched as his father reacted to the command. Lloyd appeared to shrink in on himself. "You'll just have to take my word for it," he told Miranda. "That's the best I can do."

Miranda sat back and crossed her arms. "All right. Tell me what you have."

Kane was unwillingly fascinated by the small details revealed by his parents' interaction. His father was a weak man, he realized. A handsome, charming man, but clearly a less-than-successful one who probably had chased wealth without much luck for most of his life. He was cowed by his current wife. And he'd probably found Miranda's personality equally strong. Though she didn't have the less fortunate qualities that Leeza Carter did, Miranda Fortune was nobody's pushover. As if to prove his observation, Lloyd obediently began to recount the information Miranda had requested.

"We, uh, *I* hired a private investigator to track down the twins." Lloyd smiled a little, clearly proud of himself. "Name of Sinclair, Flynn Sinclair. His father got a helping hand from your daddy years ago so he's only too happy to do a favor for the Fortunes. Sort of a payback."

"This Sinclair believes you're acting at the request of the Fortunes?"

"I figured you wouldn't want anybody to know the truth," he said. "So I told him I was representing the Fortunes."

"And?"

"And he found 'em."

Miranda waited, her only sign of tension the grip of her fingers on the arms of her chair. Kane was proud of her. She'd broken down in front of him that first day after the phone call, but she hadn't fallen apart since.

"They were raised separate," Lloyd told her. "In foster care, 'cuz they weren't adoptable."

"What do you mean, they weren't adoptable?" The news clearly agitated Miranda, and Kane put a soothing hand on her shoulder, realizing as he did so that he was mimicking Allison's unspoken methods of reassurance.

"The state said you never signed any papers giving them up. So they couldn't be adopted." This part clearly wasn't of great concern to Lloyd and he went on. "The boy's name is Justin Bond and the girl is—"

"Emma," murmured Miranda. "They kept the first names I gave them."

"Right. Emma. Michaels is her last name."

"What? Why don't they have the same last name?"

Lloyd shrugged. "Social workers. Who knows what they

were thinkin'?'' He extended a folder across the desk. ''Current photos.''

''Have you—have you met them?'' Kane could feel his mother trembling though her voice was steady.

Lloyd shook his head. ''No reason to.'' He pulled out another slip of paper. ''Here's Sinclair's phone number. He's going to contact them. He's waiting to hear from me, but when I talk to him again, I'll give him your number.''

Miranda fumbled for the handle of a desk drawer, pulling it open and extracting a cashier's check, which she slipped into an envelope and slid across the desk to Lloyd. ''There's your money. Now get out of my home.'' She got to her feet and majestically sailed from the room, her head high.

''It was good seein' you again—''

''Out.'' Kane pointed to the door, his voice very near a snarl. *''Now.* And don't come back or I'll personally make you sorry.''

Lloyd and Leeza shot to their feet, recognizing the fury in his voice as the threat it was. But as they turned toward the entrance, Lloyd turned back to Kane. ''I'm sorry you're taking this so personally. It's just business.'' There was a pleading note in his voice. ''I always dreamed we'd get a chance to know each other someday—''

''Get out!''

Allison stood in front of the leaping flames in the gas fireplace in the private family room, hugging herself with her arms. Though the temperatures outside were far from cool, she felt chilled all over.

Doors at the front of the house opened and closed, and she heard Kane's voice, sharp and angry. The front door slammed.

She couldn't stand it any longer, but as she turned to go to the door, Miranda walked into the room.

Allison was shocked. Her mother-in-law's face was drawn and pale and tears streaked uneven tracks down her cheeks. Reacting instinctively, Allison reached for her and drew Miranda into her arms, absorbing her pain as the older woman sobbed into her shoulder.

Kane appeared in the doorway, his features tight with fury. She ached to go to him, to simply put her arms around him, too, but his mother needed her more at the moment.

His gaze darkened as he saw the state Miranda was in. Stalking across to the bar, he snagged a few tissues and handed them to Allison, then silently went back to the bar, slamming two squat glasses down and splashing a generous hit of rich amber liquid into each. He lifted one and drained it in a single gulp, then stood with his hands on his hips for a long moment, his face tilted skyward.

Finally, he heaved a deep sigh and lifted the other glass, walking around the bar toward the women again.

Miranda's sobs were under control now, and she dabbed at her eyes and nose with the tissues. Allison drew her to a wing chair near the fire and Kane pressed the glass into her limp hand.

"Here," he said gruffly. "Drink."

But Miranda was fast regaining her composure. She sniffed delicately at the alcohol, then shuddered. "Ugh. Whiskey." She set the glass aside. "I'm not *that* upset, Kane." And she tried to smile.

Allison pulled a footstool over and perched at Miranda's feet. "Are you all right now?"

Miranda looked at her, and the sheer sorrow and regret in her blue eyes hit Allison like a blow. "I'm as all right as I'm going to get, I suppose." Her voice quavered, then she steadied herself with an effort. "I have the pictures of the children I gave away and the name of the investigator who's meeting with them."

Allison reached forward and placed a hand on her mother-in-law's knee, patting gently. "You were practically a child yourself. Giving them up wasn't necessarily the wrong choice. Their lives may have been the better for your decision."

"They may have been worse," Miranda said. "Apparently they were never adopted because I didn't legally sign away my parental rights."

"And I guess that's the real question," Kane said. "Do you want to find out? Do you want to contact them?"

"Yes." Miranda's voice was definite. "They are part of the Fortune family and as such are entitled to a share of my portion of that estate." She looked apologetically at Kane. "I hope that won't be—"

Kane cut her off with a curt hand motion. "You know I've never wanted any part of the family money. You can split it between Gab and these twins and leave me out of it entirely, for all I care."

Miranda smiled softly. "Yes, but you'll have children of your own someday and you may feel differently then. Anyway," her voice firmed, "I think, to be fair, that after all these years, the choice has to be theirs if they want us in their lives. After this private investigator, Flynn Sinclair, contacts each of them and tells them about their family, I'd like to extend an invitation to visit us here. I intend to respect their wishes if they choose not to contact us. After all, they may have families of their own who would be very hurt if they suddenly formed bonds with biological relatives. Or they simply may not want to get to know me. Us."

"What are you going to tell Uncle Ryan?"

His mother shrugged. "I don't know. If neither child

wants to meet me, I'll never tell him at all." Her eyes filled with tears. "I'll worry about Ryan later."

Kane drove Allison home shortly afterward. He briefly outlined the events that had occurred during the meeting with his father, including his impressions of both the Carters.

He made love to her then with the same urgency he always displayed, but she sensed that a part of him wasn't with her, that he was still caught up in the events of the evening.

Afterward, for the first time since they'd begun sleeping in the same bed, he'd moved away from her. This time he didn't gather her back into his arms to sleep, but rose from the bed.

"I'll be downstairs for a little while."

"Are you all right?" She sat up and faced him as he pulled on pajama bottoms.

He nodded. "Yeah. Just madder than hell. I wish that scumbag had died years ago."

She was genuinely shocked. "No," she said positively. "You don't."

"I do." His voice was adamant. "You don't know what it was like in there tonight, having to watch my mother deal with that pair."

"Still," she said, "dead is forever. Once someone is gone, you can never go back again."

"Exactly." He'd left the room then, and she'd finally fallen into a restless sleep. She'd wakened several hours later when he came to bed, and when he'd tucked her in against him in the position in which she usually slept now, she'd finally sighed, feeling comforted despite his odd mood.

* * *

Late the next afternoon, her period started.

Kane had gone to the hospital earlier in the day, and Allison was alone in the house. She'd been gathering a load of laundry when the familiar cramping sensation alerted her.

Slowly, she came out of the bathroom and sat on the edge of the bed. She should be relieved that she wasn't pregnant.

But…she wasn't. Tears burned at the backs of her eyes and she fiercely pressed her palms against the closed lids, refusing to howl out her disappointment. If she'd been pregnant, she would have a link to Kane forever. A person made from the two of them. And she knew Kane well enough to know that he would never set aside a family that included a child, as her father had.

No, if she'd been pregnant, there would be no question in her mind that her marriage would last. Now…without a child, using birth control to prevent a pregnancy, there was no reason for them to stay together. Oh, she knew what he'd said, several times, about this marriage being a permanent thing. But she also knew that she didn't have what it took to keep Kane interested in her for long, no matter how attentive he'd been yesterday and last night.

Though he seemed enthralled with her in bed, he was often cool and moody outside of it. When the sexual attraction wore off for him, that would be the end.

You're being melodramatic and silly, she told herself. *Just because your own father behaved like that doesn't mean Kane will.*

But as hard as she tried to be positive, that one tiny doubt couldn't be erased. If her pretty, charming mother hadn't been able to hold a man's interest, how likely was it that she, plain quiet Allison, could do so?

The ringing of the telephone cut off her momentary pessimism and she stood, reaching for the handset.

"Fortune residence, Allison speaking." The words still gave her a thrill.

"Good afternoon. This is Lloyd Carter. May I speak to Kane?"

She nearly dropped the receiver as she realized she was speaking to Kane's father. "I'm sorry, Mr. Carter. Kane isn't available right now."

"Are you his wife?"

"Yes, sir. May I take a message?"

Lloyd Carter hesitated in response to her question. "Well, I guess you can just tell him I called and ask him to return the call. Tell him I'd like to take him to dinner, have a chance to talk."

"Thank you, Mr. Carter. I'll be sure to give him the message." Although she could imagine the reaction it was likely to provoke.

"You'd be welcome to join us." His voice warmed. "I'd like to get to know my son's wife."

"I'll tell Kane," she repeated, not knowing what else to say. "Is there a number where he can reach you?"

As the man reeled off a local number, she wrote it down automatically, wondering if there was any chance at all that Kane might be willing to talk with his father. Mr. Carter sounded sincere. And though she abhorred the blackmail to which he'd resorted, she'd also heard Kane's speculation about the unpleasant Mrs. Carter and her role in the whole plan. Was it possible Lloyd Carter had been manipulated? She wondered, also, what kind of reason he might give for his disappearance from his young family's lives all those years ago.

She knew better than most how draining it could be to carry a grudge, to nurse anger and pain instead of letting go of the past. On impulse, she pulled the box of her family photos out of the closet where Kane had stored it. She studied the grainy photograph of her father's face. He'd tried to talk to her about his own leave-taking numerous times, and each time she'd cut him off. He'd died still trying to win her forgiveness, and she hadn't realized how badly she needed to give it until it was too late.

Pain lanced through her, and she pushed the snapshot out of the way as hot tears of regret splashed down her cheeks. Maybe she could make Kane see how futile it was to hate his father. Maybe she could help him to avoid the lifelong regret she'd always carry.

Kane let himself in quietly, knowing Allison had probably gone to bed several hours ago. He hadn't needed to stay so long at the hospital, but he'd done it anyway, hoping that he wouldn't have to face her tonight.

She was just too damned tempting.

It was ridiculous to want any woman the way he wanted her. He could smell her scent in every breath he took, hear her voice in his mind throughout his waking moments. His fingers tingled at the thought of stroking her satiny skin, and his body began to respond to the mere thought of holding her against him.

His blood was pounding through his veins, and he was sweating slightly as he walked up the stairs and entered the bedroom. Annoyed with himself, he refused to glance at the bed as he emptied his pockets and shed his clothing, then headed for the bathroom.

A few minutes later, he slipped into his side of the big bed. His wife was an indistinct blur in the darkness, but her scent clung to the pillows and sheets, making his body react uncomfortably.

"You're late tonight."

Her quiet voice startled him. Annoyed at the accusation he perceived, too aware of her soft skin only inches away, he growled, "I'm a doctor. I work as long as there are patients who need my help."

He felt the sheets drag across him as she recoiled from his harsh tone. "I only meant—"

"You knew when you married me I wasn't a nine-to-five kind of guy."

There was a long silence in the bedroom. She didn't move. Guilt began to creep in around the edges of his irritation. Then she spoke again.

"I'm sorry." Her voice quavered. "I was worried that you'd had a bad day, and I thought you might need to talk."

Well, hell. He'd misunderstood her words. What was he supposed to say? He heard a sniff and fresh guilt speared him. Was she crying? He took a deep breath, resisting the instinct that called him to pull her into his arms. Letting out a gusty sigh, he said, "I apologize, too. I had a tough day, but that was no reason to take it out on you." He forced himself to turn onto his side facing away from her. "Good night."

"Good night." She was definitely crying, although he could tell from her careful breathing that she was trying not to let him know it.

He lay rigid in the darkness as her breathing eventually evened out into the patterns of slumber. It had taken every ounce of willpower he had not to turn and reach across the space that divided them and haul her into his arms. He didn't know exactly what he'd expected of this marriage when he'd initially thought about it, but he did know he'd never expected to be fighting *himself* most of the time.

She was already up and dressed, probably for several hours, when he awoke the next day. Dragging on a pair of sweat shorts, he washed his face and tore a comb through his unruly hair before padding down the stairs and into the kitchen.

"Good morning." Allison was seated at the kitchen table. Looking up, she offered him a wary smile. "Would you like me to make you some eggs?"

Remembering his foul humor of the night before, he couldn't believe she was even speaking to him, much less smiling. "That would be great." It wasn't until he'd poured himself a cup of coffee and rounded the counter that he saw she had her box of family photos out. "What are you doing?"

"Just sorting through some stuff. I need to put these in albums." Her head was buried in the refrigerator. "Um, Kane?"

"Hmm?" He picked up one of the photos and glanced at the date on the back.

"I started my period yesterday. We're not going to be parents."

Slowly, he set down the photo and turned to face her, but she had her back to him, cracking eggs into the skillet and laying strips of bacon in a frying pan. "Well, that's good news." He tried to make his voice hearty. It *was* good news, wasn't it? For the best? They needed time to get this marriage thing worked out before they added children to the mix. After last night that should be crystal clear. Still, he knew a mild regret and that in itself surprised him. Had he *wanted* Allison to be pregnant? The answer to that was too complex to confront first thing in the morning.

"I can go on the pill now." She still wasn't looking at him.

He was silent for a moment, thinking about it. Logically, that would be the thing to do. And it would free him from the conscious interruption that male protection necessitated during sex. But... "Let me think about it. Don't do anything yet." He peered into his coffee cup as if it held answers to questions he didn't know how to ask. "We'll talk later about our plans for children, all right?"

She nodded, and there was an odd stiff silence, broken only by the sizzle and pop of the frying bacon.

"There's a message on the table for you. A phone call from last night." Allison appeared to have dismissed the topic of pregnancy easily; he assumed she was relieved.

"Who's it from?" Idly, he reached for the slip of yellow paper.

"Your father."

"What?" He dropped the paper as if it were burning him. "What the hell did that blackmailing bastard want?" He was so agitated he sprang to his feet and paced the length of the kitchen.

Allison turned, her eyes huge and concerned. "He only wanted to talk to you. He invited you—both of us, actually—to dinner. I think he wants to get to know you."

He made a rude suggestion as to what his father could do with his dinner. "No way are we meeting with him," he said flatly. "God only knows what other schemes he has up his sleeve."

"You said you weren't sure the blackmailing idea was his," Allison reminded him. "And what could it hurt to meet with him one time? He's the only father you have."

"No." It wasn't an option. "I grew up without him just fine. I'll stay fatherless. That piece of slime will never have a place in my life. If he calls again, hang up. I don't want you talking to him." To emphasize that the conversation was ended, he resumed his seat and took a deliberate drink of his coffee. Then he picked up one of the photos lying before him at random, more to distract her than because he was really interested. "This looks like the other picture you showed me of *your* father. But that's not your mother. Did he remarry?''

''Yes. That was the second of his wives.'' She slipped his omelet onto a plate and began to fork bacon onto it as he studied the snapshot.

Kane was startled by the way she phrased it; he lifted his head and stared at her back. ''How many wives did he have?''

''He was on number four when he died.'' Allison's voice was devoid of any inflection. No sarcasm, no humor, no pain, no…nothing. She wasn't usually so expressionless and that alone was enough to warn him that this was a sensitive topic.

''Tell me again when your parents split up?'' This guy sounded like a real winner.

''He left us when I was twelve.''

Us. Not ''her,'' not ''my mother,'' but ''us.'' Something flickered at the back of his mind, but it refused to focus enough for him to get a grip on the thought. After a moment, he said, ''So what did you think of the other wives?''

Allison shrugged. ''I never met any of them except for the last one. Dad and I didn't communicate much after he left. The last wife and I spoke briefly at the funeral. She seemed…decent. She invited me to come by their house sometimes. She wanted me to have anything of his that I wanted.''

''Why didn't you meet any of the others? Were you already on your own by the time he remarried?''

She snorted. ''Hardly. He married number two a week after his divorce from Mama was final. We saw the notice in the paper. That lasted about a year, then he ditched her and married number three. That one lasted longer, but about eight years ago, number three bit the dust, too.'' She gave him a humorless smile. ''Funny, huh?''

Kane shook his head. "Sad. So when did he meet the last one?"

"I'm not sure. She gave me the impression they hadn't been married too long—not years and years, or anything like that. In fact, I assume she was the fourth wife. For all I know, there could have been more in between there. Just because it wasn't in the paper doesn't mean anything. I assumed he always lived in San Antonio, but I could be wrong."

"And you weren't in touch with him at all, ever, after he left?" He'd seen firsthand what it was like to be cut off from your family. His mother's joy when her brother had welcomed her back had been as great as her regret at waiting so long and missing the end of her father's life. What had Allison thought, what had she felt during all those years? Abandoned. Ignored. Forgotten. Feelings no child should ever have to face.

He'd faced them and still bore his own scars. Although how much worse had it been for her? His father had never been in his life so he didn't really know what he was missing; his life had seemed relatively complete. Her father, in contrast, had been there for a dozen years before suddenly vanishing without, as it appeared, a word to his young daughter.

"No, we weren't in touch immediately." She sighed as she set down his breakfast before him.

The sound was so full of sorrow and hopelessness that he reached for her hand despite his resolve not to touch her unnecessarily. "Sounds like you would have liked to have been."

"Not then, I wouldn't have." Her palm turned up and she clasped his fingers as if he'd thrown her a lifeline. "He contacted me several times in the years after he left. I always refused to talk to him. He tried again after I graduated from high school. Said he'd like to get together, to get to know me, to apologize for his actions and try to explain. But I...I refused. I never let him have that chance. I never gave him a single crumb. Not even one little meeting.''

And yet she'd kept all those crystal cats her father had collected for her. Maybe she hadn't been able to forgive him, but she'd cared.

She released her grip on his fingers and clasped her hands together. "I regret being so stubborn now.''

"Why?''

She shrugged. "He's the only father I had. And I have no idea what his motivations were for the choices he made in his life. He genuinely wanted to rebuild his bridges with me, I believe. But I couldn't get past my anger. And before I did, he died.''

"How did he die?''

"Suddenly. He had a massive heart attack one day and that was that.''

"I'm sorry." He felt awkward—how was he supposed to respond to that? She wasn't being very subtle. He knew she was trying to tell him he should cut his own old man some slack. But her situation had been different. Lloyd Carter and he had nothing to talk about. Ever. If the man died tomorrow, he wouldn't be sorry.

Kane picked up his fork and began to cut into the fluffy omelet, avoiding her eyes. When he finally glanced at her, though, she didn't say anything else. The silence grew oppressive and he felt her silent reproach. He'd disappointed her.

Well, it was none of her business. But...it bothered him that he'd upset her. Allison had always been there to soothe and comfort him. It was unsettling to acknowledge how badly he needed her approval.

Seven

He took her shopping later in the day. Allison protested, saying that there was nothing that she needed. But he knew better. He did a minimum of socializing with the Fortune family en masse, but there were occasions when his presence was requested and he wanted her to feel confident.

As he was heading off McCullough Avenue into the parking lots of the North Star Mall, Allison snapped her fingers. "I forgot to tell you—your mother also called last night. She said it was no big deal, but she sounded strange. You probably should check in with her today."

"Maybe we'll swing by her place when we're finished here," he said. "Unless you get into the shopping thing a whole lot more than you seem to be, I predict we'll be out of here within two hours."

He was right. In fact, they never even made it out of the mall's department store except for a brief excursion to a specialty shoe shop. She bought one evening dress, two suits with skirts, two trim pants suits and a slim, sexy coat dress that he loved, largely because with a flick of a few buttons, he could have her naked. Though he didn't tell her that. The sales people were only too happy to show her numerous accessories and she chose scarves, pins, necklaces and earrings with swift and tasteful efficiency.

They drove to his mother's house afterward, largely just to check on her. Though she was the strongest woman he knew, Kane still worried about the effects of the shattering meeting of a few days before on her spirits.

Miranda met them at the door and he saw immediately that he'd been worrying for no reason. Her cheeks were pink and her eyes sparkled. And though she still clearly carried around her concerns, he was reassured.

"Hello, darlings! Can you stay?" She threw open the door.

He shook his head. "Just for a few minutes. We both have to work today."

Miranda made a face. "You two work harder than anyone I know. Medicine's a very demanding field, isn't it?"

Allison nodded. "I do love my work but the long shifts can be grueling."

"Just wait 'til you have babies of your own," Miranda commented. "Being on duty twenty-four hours a day—*that's* grueling." She smiled at her son. "But you'll have Kane to help you."

There was a short awkward silence. Could his mother have picked a worse topic of conversation? "Allison said you called yesterday."

Miranda's smile dimmed immediately. "I did. I have some news about the twins." She stopped and took a deep breath. "The private investigator is bringing them to San Antonio next weekend. I've invited them to stay here."

Kane felt the bottom drop out of his stomach. It was one

thing to learn about his siblings; it was another entirely to meet them face-to-face. His first impulse was to protest. *But I don't want to!* His second impulse was to laugh grimly at himself. *Baby.*

"And have you heard from them?" Allison covered his silence quickly and he realized gratefully that, as usual, she was protecting him.

Miranda shook her head. "Mr. Sinclair should be calling me later today. I'll let you know as soon as we firm up the dates and we'll arrange to get together. I know you'll want to meet them."

It was the first time in his memory that his mother had been so completely wrong about what he was thinking.

"Oh, I almost forgot," his mother added. "I told your Uncle Ryan about the twins and their upcoming visit."

"What did he say?" Again, Kane had the sensation of events spinning out of his control. If his mother was sharing the information with the other Fortunes, it meant that these two people were definitely going to enter his life, like it or not.

"He was...very supportive." Miranda's eyes were moist and she patted the back of the hand Allison laid on her arm. "He won't mention it to the rest of the family until after we've met them. Depending on the outcome of our meeting, there may be no need to mention anything at all."

The next week went far too fast, as far as Kane was concerned. On Saturday morning, he rose before the sun and went down to his workout equipment for nearly an hour, then climbed into the shower. Allison was still sleeping.

She had to work today so he would be on his own with this visit. A part of him wanted to run the opposite direction, to stick his head in the sand and pretend everything was the way it used to be.

Only it wasn't. And it would never be again. For him, "the way it used to be" meant his mother, his sister and him. The Three Musketeers. Or the Three Stooges, depending on your point of view, he thought fondly. They'd had some pretty good times, despite the ever-present lack of money.

He supposed he should be taking the sudden appearance of this brother and sister in stride. After all, what were two more faces compared to the myriad he'd already met? But these weren't just two more relatives. These were his half siblings. His own mother's children. He supposed the bottom line was that he was a little jealous. Worried that he'd be replaced in his mother's affections. Like a stupid kid.

Why should he be worried? He'd cut the apron strings. He even had a wife of his own now. The thought immediately distracted him from thinking of his mother.

He scowled into the mirror as he shaved. He'd deliberately worked long hours in the past week, trying to exhaust himself as well as trying to stay as far from his wife as possible. According to his mental timetable, her period should be well over by now, but he hadn't made love to her again.

He didn't need her, he told himself for about the millionth time. Sure, it was *nice* being married to her, but it wasn't like he couldn't live without her.

If you're so sure of that, then why are you denying yourself? You want her so bad you can taste it.

Sheer physical attraction, he reminded himself. Stronger by far than anything he'd ever felt for any other woman, but still, just physical attraction. Nothing he couldn't control.

Right.

He scowled at his reflection again. Who was he kidding?

As if his imagination had produced her, the bathroom door opened and Allison walked in, her hair a wild cornsilk halo around her head, curls streaming over the straps of her skimpy black gown. "Oh, sorry," she said. "Good morning. I thought you were downstairs." She smiled sleepily at him as she reached for a washcloth and scrubbed her face. "I need a shower, but I can wait until you're done."

She turned to leave.

But the heavy-lidded, sleepy smile had cut the fine thread holding his self-control in check. "Allison." He caught her hand before she could go.

She turned, eyebrows raised.

Using their clasped hands, he tugged her to him in one quick motion. She stumbled smack into him and he immediately snaked his arms around her back, locking her in place. "You can shower with me." His voice was deep and raspy, even more than the early hour warranted.

The radiant smile that pleased him so much lit her face, and she lifted her arms to circle his neck. "You've got a deal, doctor."

The shower water was hot on his back. Allison writhed in his arms, pinned to the cool tile wall by his surging body. He battled his own climax long enough to feel her sweet inner muscles grabbing at him before he lost the fight and poured himself into her, groaning aloud as his seed jetted from him—

"Oh, hell," he said. "Guess what we just did?"

She chuckled. "I don't think I have to guess."

"Very funny. I meant birth control."

She lifted her head from where she'd dropped it against his shoulder, and he could see the aftermath of her pleasure glowing in her eyes. "The timing's wrong. We're probably safe.'' She contracted herself around him, and he sucked in a harsh breath of delight at the sensation. ''And it feels so good this way, doesn't it?''

''That it does.'' He lifted her off him and reached an arm over the shower stall door for two thick bath sheets. ''I vote we adjourn to the bedroom.''

She smiled. ''Okay. Or should I say, 'Yea'?'' She preceded him out the bathroom door. But his eye caught the clock as they approached the bed.

''Damn.'' He pulled her to a stop. ''You'll be late for work.''

She dropped her towel, then worked his away from his waist and dropped both to the floor, pressing her bare body against his. ''No, I won't. I traded at the last minute yesterday. I'm going to work the night shift. I thought you might want some moral support today.''

He stood stock-still as he absorbed her words.

She stepped a pace away and looked up at his face, doubt flickering in her expressive eyes. ''But if you'd rather meet them alone, I understand. I just thought—''

''Thank you.'' He pulled her close again and found her mouth with his. ''I'd like to have you with me.'' That sounded too needy to his ears, so he forced a smile before he reclaimed her lips. ''Just in case I get the urge to do this again.''

When the dark-colored rental sedan pulled into the driveway of Melrose Manor, Allison thought she could have cut the tension in the air with the dull kitchen shears she'd found in one of Kane's kitchen drawers when she'd moved in. The four of them had automatically moved out onto the flagstone porch to welcome their guests, but the silence didn't exactly feel welcoming.

She glanced at Miranda. The older woman was clearly

very nervous, clenching and unclenching her clasped hands and biting her lower lip. Kane and his sister were both still, in contrast. Both somber. Both, she thought, probably feeling a bit threatened by this whole thing, even if they were adults who didn't require their mother's physical care anymore. It would be immensely unnerving to learn that you were going to be sharing your mother with two complete strangers who had as much right to her affection as you did.

The sedan braked to a halt, and the driver's side door opened. A dark-haired man unfolded himself from the seat and came around the car with his hand extended. "Mrs. Fortune? Flynn Sinclair. Glad I could be of help in bringing this reunion about."

Miranda took his hand, but her attention was focused on another man, tall, also dark-haired, emerging from the car. He wore a conservative dark suit. Everything about him, from the well-groomed dark hair to the tips of his expensive black loafers, shouted that this man was a success. He gave the assembled group a swift, assessing look out of laser-blue eyes, then dismissed them in the same moment to give his attention to the woman to whom he'd extended his hand. She was much shorter than he, shorter than any of them, dark-haired like her twin, although her hair was shoulder-length and wisps of curl waved around her face. She wore sandals and a loose gauzy dress that was as inexpensive as her twin's attire was costly. And as she moved from behind the car door, Allison heard Miranda give a soft gasp. The girl was pregnant. Quite pregnant.

Sinclair, the private investigator whom Lloyd Carter had hired under false pretenses, reached out to draw the pair closer, his hand hovering protectively at the young woman's back. "Mrs. Fortune, this is Emma Michaels."

The pregnant woman stepped forward. Miranda spontaneously threw out both arms but the other woman reacted quickly, thrusting out a hand and shaking Miranda's once before backing off. "It's..." she hesitated. "....*interesting* to meet you, Mrs. Fortune," she said with a wry smile that revealed a dimple in her left cheek.

Must be from her father's side, Allison thought. The twins shared more than simply that dimple. Though Justin was significantly taller than his sister, there was a distinct resemblance in their coloring and their features, especially around the eyes...eyes that were carbon copies of Miranda's blue orbs, she realized with a shock. Neither Kane nor Gabrielle had gotten their mother's eye color. Still, the four siblings shared an eerie familial quality.

"Miranda. Please call me Miranda." Kane's mother's eyes were shiny with tears.

"This is Justin Bond." Emma turned and indicated the watchful dark-haired man a pace behind her.

Miranda had regrouped as she spoke and recovered her social mask. With the flawless manners she usually displayed, she gave Justin a very appropriate, brief handshake. "It's very nice to meet you both," she said. She turned to indicate the trio ranged just behind and to her left. "This is my daughter Gabrielle Grayhawk, my son Kane Fortune and his wife, Allison."

There was yet another excruciatingly polite round of handshakes and meaningless murmurs. When those had concluded, everyone looked at Miranda again.

She bit her lip. "Why don't you all come inside and we'll continue this with some cool drinks and lunch?"

The whole group trooped inside in silence. As they moved through the house, Allison noted that Emma was looking around in awe, clearly unused to the level of wealth so casually enjoyed by her mother. Justin, on the other hand, didn't appear to be nearly as impressed. Miranda led them out to the shaded terrace where a light buffet had been set up. Just beyond, the blue waters of the inground pool sparkled beneath the Texas sun, comfortably warm even in early February.

Miranda poured drinks and handed them around while Flynn Sinclair spoke quietly to her. Gabrielle hovered protectively at her mother's elbow. The twins stuck close together, Allison noted, walking out into the sunshine to look at the pool. They obviously had met before this morning because they appeared to be relatively comfortable with each other—and as clearly uncomfortable with the idea of embracing any additional family members.

Snagging a glass of lemonade, she approached the pair. "Welcome to San Antonio," she said. "The climate can't be beat this time of year."

"It's certainly a change from Pennsylvania," said Justin.

"I imagine so. You'll have to go downtown while you're here. San Antonio is a charming city."

"I doubt I'll be doing much sight-seeing. I have a flight out tomorrow." Justin lifted his drink to his lips.

"That's awfully soon." Kane had come up beside her. "We'd hoped you'd stay for a few days."

Justin shook his head. "Business calls."

And it's a good excuse, Allison thought. She supposed she couldn't blame him. "I guess this is quite a shock, finding not only your birth mother but a twin and lots of other relatives."

"Famous ones, at that," Emma put in.

Allison smiled. "If it's any consolation, I can identify in a small way. Kane and I just married a week ago. I'm still easily overwhelmed by all the Fortunes running around. Not to mention all the money running around with them."

Kane nodded. "It can be overwhelming."

"But you must be used to it. You're one of them…a Fortune," said Emma.

"You're one of them now, too." Kane chuckled, smiling, and Allison marveled at how easily he turned on the charm. But she wasn't fooled. Standing close enough to him that their arms brushed, she could feel the nervous tension practically vibrating through him. "And no, I'm not that used to it. Until just a few years ago, I didn't know I was a Fortune, either."

"What does that mean?" Justin was definitely the tougher nut of the twosome. If he'd smiled yet, Allison hadn't seen it. Would he look more like Kane, or less, if he ever did smile?

"It meant exactly what it sounded like." Kane's voice was easy. "Mother was estranged from the family when she was a teenager. Gabrielle and I grew up without knowing of the Fortune connection. In fact, it's only been about six years since we were welcomed into the family." He smiled again. "It'll be kind of fun to watch someone else trying make sense of the whole crazy clan."

"That's assuming we decide we *want* to be welcomed in to the family," Justin said.

"True." Kane's smile faded. He shifted to face his half brother squarely. "I hope you'll give Mother a chance. Let her explain the circumstances surrounding your birth."

Justin nodded noncommittally. His expression was unreadable. "I look forward to hearing it."

"So," said Allison, trying to ease the tension that had reappeared with Justin's cool words. "Justin is from Pennsylvania. Where are you from, Emma?" Miranda was approaching across the terrace with the investigator Sinclair trailing behind her. Allison didn't want the older woman to hear them discussing her behind her back.

"I've been living in New Mexico." The petite brunette

rubbed a hand over her swollen belly and shifted as if she were uncomfortable. "But I won't be returning there."

"Oh? Where will you be going?" Miranda asked as she joined them. The way she looked from one twin to the other and back again was heartbreaking to watch, as if she were trying to store up a lifetime of memories in a few moments.

Emma hesitated. "I haven't really decided yet."

"But surely you must have plans. What does your husband want to do?" Miranda looked shocked. "You can't be far from your delivery date."

"There is no husband," Emma said. Allison had to admire the easy acceptance in her voice. If she were in Emma's shoes, pregnant and apparently alone, she'd be a basket case. "I have a little while to make plans."

Kane snorted. "That's a recipe for an early delivery if I ever heard one. Don't wait too long. Babies aren't very predictable."

Emma's face registered her surprise at his knowledgeable voice.

"Kane's a doctor. He specializes in pre-term babies," Allison explained.

Emma's eyebrows rose and she smiled broadly. "Then I'm in good hands if I go into labor today, hmm?"

Kane made an expression of exaggerated horror. "I certainly hope that doesn't happen. But if it should, you are indeed in good hands. Allison is a pediatric nurse. In fact, we met at the hospital."

"Oh, that must have been romantic."

Kane's eyes caught hers in amusement. Allison smiled at him, wondering if he was thinking of incubators and intravenous lines as she was. *Romantic* wasn't the term she'd have picked.

Miranda's eyes had been far away as the conversation wove around her. Into the lull that followed Emma's response to Kane's words, she said, "So you don't have definite plans, Emma? Because if you have the time and you'd like to visit, I'd love to have you stay here for as long as you like."

Allison could see immediate refusal rising in the younger woman's face. Hastily, she said, "Don't decide now. Take some time and think about it." She turned to Miranda. "I think Emma needs to get out of this sun. Why don't we eat?"

The meal went far more easily than she'd expected. Kane went out of his way to set his siblings at ease, telling stories about his work at the hospital. Gabrielle showed off pictures of her daughter, and Flynn Sinclair responded tolerantly to her questions about the art of investigation. It was surface conversation, but she sensed it was what the twins needed as they absorbed the impact of this new situation.

Finally Kane rose. He eyed the door and Allison immediately caught on. Setting down her napkin, she rose as well.

"Thank you for the meal, Mother," he said as he walked around to kiss her cheek. "We have to get going. Allison and I don't often have days off at the same time, and we have things to take care of."

Justin and Flynn both stood. Emma began to rise but before she could, Kane placed his hands on her shoulders and gently pressed her back into her seat. "No, don't get up," he said. He bent and brushed a kiss along her cheek. "It's great to meet you."

Emma's hands rose and she clutched his hands where they rested on her shoulders. "Thank you. You've made this much easier than I imagined it would be."

Kane went around the table then, shaking the men's hands while Allison said her farewells. Moments later, he helped her into the Explorer and they headed home.

He didn't seem to want to talk on the drive, and she respected his privacy. He clearly was troubled and the taut line of his lips drew thinner and thinner as the silence grew heavier and heavier.

He flopped down heavily in his large recliner the moment they were home.

Allison went to the kitchen and made them each a cup of coffee. Bringing his to him, she set hers down on an end table and walked around behind the chair. She set her hands on the tense muscles of his neck and shoulders, humming disapprovingly at what she found. "This feels like concrete."

Quietly, she began to knead his muscles, digging her thumbs into the tight knots and holding pressure on them until the cramps relaxed. Kane sighed under her ministrations. He moaned. He groaned occasionally when she hit a particularly touchy spot. He leaned forward to give her better access to his back and drew his shirt over his head so that her hands cruised over his bare flesh.

She slipped around and settled herself on one arm of the chair, still massaging. Her fingers slid up into his hair and rubbed over his scalp repeatedly, then she made gentle circles at his temples before turning her attention to his back again.

He felt good beneath her hands, so good that she couldn't help but want him and she shifted on the arm of the chair as she became aroused. Her body ached to press against his but she couldn't bring herself to initiate lovemaking. If he rejected her attentions, she'd die. Still, she couldn't resist lowering her head and brushing gentle, open-mouthed kisses along his spine.

Kane shot straight upright. He made a sound deep in his throat as he stood and reached for her, drawing her against him. They both groaned.

"Thank you. That felt great." His breathing was fast and harsh in her ear. "This feels even better." His hands moved to the buttons and hooks on the simple dress she'd worn to lunch and in seconds it fluttered down around her ankles. The dress had a halter-style top so she wasn't wearing a bra and, as he looked down at her pretty breasts nestled in the palms of his big hands, a dark flush of desire rose high on his cheekbones.

He dragged his belt open and tore at the fastenings of his pants, shoving them down just far enough to draw her against his hot, naked body, holding her hard against the powerfully aroused flesh at his groin and grinding himself against her. "I want you," he growled, dragging her backward to the couch.

Moments later they drove steadily toward a heaving, tumultuous climax that left her shivering in his arms.

She slumped forward, her head bowed and her forehead resting against his throat while his chin brushed the top of her head while they both gasped for air. Then, while she was still limp and pliant, Kane thrust a big hand through her hair and cradled the back of her scalp, turning her face up to his.

He kissed her. The kiss was surprisingly sweet, intimate and open in a way he hadn't been before. She couldn't have put it into words, but there was something different. Then he raised his head a fraction, dragging his lips from hers. "Allison…" He hesitated for a moment.

"Yes?" She felt as if she were on the verge of some stunning new discovery.

"You love me, don't you?" His eyes were a blazing green as they bored into hers.

She fell off the edge of the precipice on which she'd been balancing. Her eyes closed. Would he be angry if she said yes? Instinctively, she began to withdraw mentally, wondering how she could smooth it over. Had she said it aloud during their lovemaking? She didn't remember.

"Allison?" He shook her lightly and she opened her eyes apprehensively. He was smiling, a slightly crooked, diffident expression. "Do you love me?"

"I—" That smile sealed her fate. Casting common sense to the winds, she whispered, "Yes."

"Say it."

"I love you." She searched his eyes, wondering what was going through that complicated brain of his, but all she saw was satiated pleasure.

"Good," he said with satisfaction. "I thought you did." He drew her close against his chest again, snagging a lap blanket from the back of the couch and draping it over her bare back. He yawned. "I'm glad."

Neither of them spoke again for a long while. She hadn't ever expected to hear him say that he loved her, so she wasn't disappointed…at least that's what she told herself. It would have to be enough that he'd accepted her love. After all, she'd never even dared to hope that she'd be married to him, so their new closeness was merely icing on the cake. Of course it was.

Kane napped. At least he thought he did. When he opened his eyes again, Allison was still snuggled in his arms and he was still embedded deep within her. Experimentally, he moved his hips a fraction and was rewarded as her inner muscles contracted briefly around him. He sucked his breath in in reaction. How in the hell could he feel like this again so soon?

He felt her lips move as she formed a soft kiss against his breastbone. "Was that an invitation?"

He laughed. He couldn't help it. Damned if she didn't make him happy. Why hadn't he married her years ago?

And why had he been fighting this so hard? "Yeah," he confirmed. "It was. An invitation to spend the rest of the day in bed."

She sat up slowly, shaking her hair back over her shoulders, and he could feel it brush his thighs, a whole new sensory delight that opened up a whole host of new ideas. "All right," she said. "But you have to feed me."

He lifted her off him long enough to rise, then slipped his arms beneath her knees and back and swept her into his arms. "Don't worry," he said, nibbling at her kiss-swollen reddened lower lip. "I'll feed you."

By early evening, they were both too worn out to move. The remains of a turkey sub lay in a messy lump on a paper plate on the bedside table. Kane lay on his back with Allison cradled in one arm.

"I wonder if I'll be able to walk tomorrow," he said speculatively. "If my knees give out in the delivery room, they're liable to think it was the sight of blood."

"That would be preferable to other things they might think," Allison said primly.

He grinned and stroked a hand down over her frothy, disheveled curls. "I didn't thank you for today," he said, his grin fading. "You really have a knack for making people feel at ease. Your presence probably had a great deal to do with how successful that first meeting with my new sister and brother was."

"I hope it was successful," she said reflectively. "I know the whole thing has been difficult for you."

"I was jealous at first," he confessed. "A little. She's *my* mother, and the thought of her being so excited about meeting two perfect strangers bothered me. I know it isn't logical—after all, they're her babies, too—but still..."

"You wouldn't be human if you didn't feel a little threatened." She rose over him and propped her forearms on his chest, looking down into his face as her hair cascaded around them, creating a small, intimate cave. "So what did you think of them?"

"I liked them," he said slowly. "I wasn't sure I would, but once I met them, it felt…right."

"They're very different," she said. "Emma seems to be much more of a free spirit. Justin never relaxed through the whole meal."

"He was tense," Kane agreed. "I would have liked to talk to him about his work but he wasn't approachable."

"Give it time," she said. "I hope Emma will decide to stay with Miranda. Or at least stay in San Antonio. Your mother would be so thrilled."

"My mother," said Kane dryly, "is dying to get her hands on another grandchild." Then he sobered. "I really, really hope each of them will give her a chance."

They fell silent again. She moved her arms to her sides and lay half atop him; he loosely wrapped his arms around her slight frame.

It felt so right. He'd recognized it before—this feeling of rightness. And he'd fought it. Now he was having a hard time recalling just why it was so imperative that he keep his distance from her. True, he didn't accept people into his life easily. True, he'd had his mother and sister to love and thought that was enough. No love, no getting hurt.

But he'd become a different person with Allison. He'd told her things he'd never even shared with his sister, as close as they were. He could depend on her. Allison wasn't going to hurt him. She loved him. His spirits rose even higher at the memory of her soft voice telling him so over and over and over in the final moments of their last love-making. No, Allison would never hurt him. It was okay to admit to himself that he needed her. He could accept her love and treasure it and do everything in his power to make her never regret marrying him.

It didn't matter that he hadn't returned the words, he thought defensively. Love hadn't been a part of their agreement from the first. A feeling akin to panic rose at the idea of uttering those three little words. Loving her seemed a whole lot more frightening than simply admitting he needed her. And much as he regretted it, he knew he couldn't say those words to her.

Eight

On the third week after their wedding, Kane got called to the hospital only moments after Allison had arrived home in the evening. Disappointed that their time together had been cut short, Allison wandered into the den and thumbed through the television guide listlessly.

They'd been planning an early evening. Since Kane was on call, they were holding off on opening a new bottle of chardonnay, but it wouldn't have mattered. Wine or no wine, the evening would have ended in a perfect way, with her right where she wanted to be. In her husband's arms.

She frowned slightly. Perhaps she should say almost perfect. In a perfect world, Kane would love her as much as she loved him.

He'd been a different man since the night she'd told him of her love, less aloof, warmer and more physically affectionate. It seemed as if he'd relaxed some sort of invisible barrier he'd been keeping between them. He held her hand, toyed with her hair, brushed her lips with a kiss before he left her. He made love to her even more often than he had before. There hadn't been a night that she hadn't slept in his arms exhausted unless one of them had to work.

Like tonight.

She looked forward to the times when they shared a bed so much it was absolutely pathetic, she thought. The mere thought of his hands on her body made her breath come faster. His lovemaking verged on being out of control each time he touched her, his actions hurried and rushed until he had her naked beneath him with her hair down and his body snugly buried within her. Then and only then did he slow himself down, touching and caressing her until she flew apart in his arms. If he made love to her more than once, the second time was usually less urgent, and he lingered over her, making her so frantic for him that she had to beg him to end her torment.

But he had never, in any way, indicated that he returned her feelings. And she told herself it wasn't fair to expect more—she'd known what she was getting into when she'd married him. Still…

The telephone rang. Eagerly she reached for the receiver. Each time the phone rang while Kane was gone she hoped it was him; it rarely was. Some things hadn't changed—he apparently didn't think of her when he wasn't with her. Still, hope soared as she opened the connection.

"Hello, Allison? This is Miranda."

Allison sat up straighter on the couch. "Hi. How are you?" Her mother-in-law had been on Cloud Nine since the day after the reunion luncheon, when Emma had accepted her offer of a temporary home.

"I'm fine, dear. So is Emma, although she's exhausted. We went shopping today. All her clothing was getting too tight."

"Has she gone to an obstetrician yet?" Both Kane and Allison had been insistent that Emma find a local obstetrician immediately. They'd seen too many pre-term babies whose conditions were a direct result of inadequate prenatal care.

"She made an appointment for tomorrow morning. I'm going along if she'll let me, so I can hear what this doctor has to say."

"Good." That was a relief.

"Is Kane at home? I need to speak with him."

Allison explained about the emergency that had called him out earlier. "Can I give him a message?"

Miranda hesitated. "No. Just ask him to stop by or call me as soon as possible."

When Allison turned off the phone she was thoughtful. Her mother-in-law was clearly troubled.

Before she could set the portable phone back in its cradle, it rang again, startling her so that she almost dropped it. "Fortune residence. This is Allison."

"Allison. This is Lloyd. You remember? Lloyd Carter, Kane's father."

"Hello, Mr. Carter. Yes, I remember." As if any of them would ever forget him, she thought wryly. "I'm sorry, but Kane isn't here. May I take a message?"

"Did you tell him I called before? What did he say?"

Allison hesitated. The eagerness in the man's voice was pathetic. She wasn't about to repeat exactly what Kane had said. "I told him," she said gently. "Mr. Carter, Kane isn't really interested in talking to you right now." She crossed her fingers at the little white lie. Or ever.

"I know." Carter's tone was subdued. "I really want to…to explain about leaving. I know it looks bad, but I sure do wish he'd give me a chance."

"There's also the issue of the twins and the money."

She couldn't bring herself to say the ugly word *blackmail*. "He's, um, quite upset about that."

"Doggone it. I told Leeza that was a bad idea." A tinge of annoyance crept in. "The money didn't mean all that much to me. I've been down on my luck before and something always came along. Something legal," he stressed. "Allison, you gotta help me."

"Me?" She was startled and dismayed.

"You're his wife. You know him better 'n' anybody. He's more likely to listen to you."

She wanted to deny it, to explain that just because she said it didn't mean Kane would listen, but Carter was still talking, and she couldn't find an opening.

"…Would you meet me somewhere? Let me explain it to you, so you can maybe talk to him for me, soften him up a little? I don't want to live the rest of my days without knowing my son."

She was silent. Common sense told her not to get involved in the estrangement between Kane and his father—

"Please?" There was a wealth of longing in his voice.

"All right," she said reluctantly. She really didn't like to go behind Kane's back like this, but…he was Kane's father. And she just knew Kane would regret it someday if he never gave his father a chance. Maybe this would give her some idea of how to respond to Kane's attitude. "Just for a few minutes. There's a diner down the street from the hospital. I could meet you there the day after tomorrow."

"Thank you!" It was heartfelt.

Quickly, she gave him the name of the diner and directions. They agreed on a time, and she hung up with Lloyd Carter's jubilant thanks still echoing in her ears.

Allison was nearly two hours past her usual homecoming time the next day. Kane met her at the door, a question in his eyes.

She answered him before he could voice it. "One of the Vieger quads had a diaphragmatic hernia. Cooper did the surgery. He was still hanging in there when I left, but I'll be surprised if he makes it through the night."

The family hadn't been Kane's patients, but she knew he had assisted at the delivery and was aware of the case. He sighed and shook his head. "Poor little guy. I hope he survives."

He took her bag and jacket and tossed them on a chair, then led her into the kitchen. "Hungry? I had tacos. Want me to reheat some of it?"

She shook her head. "I grabbed a sandwich a couple of hours ago. Lucky for me."

"Okay." Kane had the oddest look on his face. It was anticipation, she realized suddenly. And it wasn't just his eyes. His whole body practically vibrated with it.

Her eyes narrowed. "What's going on?"

His brows rose. "What makes you think something's going on?" But he grinned.

She grinned back. "I never realized you were so bad at keeping secrets."

"You haven't learned my secret, though, have you?" He was smug.

She spread her hands. "Are you going to keep me in suspense?"

"Not for much longer." He whipped a snowy napkin from a drawer and folded it into a rough triangle. "Here. You have to be blindfolded for this." He carefully tied the fabric behind her head, then put his hands on her shoulders. "Stay right here for a second."

"A second?" She listened to his footsteps as he rapidly crossed the kitchen and opened the door of the laundry room. "This must not be much of a surprise if it only takes a second to set it up."

"Ha." He returned and stood right in front of her. "Are you ready?"

She nodded.

"Any guesses?"

She thought for a moment. "Jewelry."

"Nope."

"Clothing."

"Your categories are too broad; you're cheating." He chuckled. "But you aren't even close."

Not even close? What in the world—

"Put out your hands."

Obediently, she outstretched her hands.

And when he carefully set a small, wriggling bundle of fur in her cupped palms, she squealed. "Kane! Get this blindfold off! What is it?"

He was laughing as he untied the blindfold and drew it aside.

In her palms was a tiny kitten. Long, soft fur, wide gray-blue eyes and a pale gray coat. It stood up as she watched, opened its tiny pink mouth and stretched, back arching and tiny dark-shaded tail reaching into the air like a plume.

She didn't know what to say. Couldn't say anything.

In the space between one heartbeat and the next, her eyes filled with tears and her throat grew so tight she couldn't get out a word.

Kane took one look at her, and his face registered alarm. "What's the matter? Don't you like cats? I can return it. I thought that since you had the whole crystal collection you might like one of the real thing, but I'll just take it—"

"No!" She found her voice abruptly. "No, I love it." She cuddled the kitten beneath her chin, trying to gain control of her seesawing emotions. "Is it a he or a she?"

"It's a female. She's a registered Rag Doll. She was the runt of the litter, but she was the friendliest." He put out a finger and gently stroked the kitten's tiny skull.

The kitten was purring. "She's…she's beautiful." She nuzzled her cheek against the small, soft body. "Thank you. I've never had a pet before."

"You're welcome." Kane set his hands at her waist and drew both Allison and the kitten into his embrace. "We always had a cat or two around when I was growing up. I wanted a dog, but my mother never let me get one—too expensive, too hard to take care of, all those motherly objections that really mean, 'No way. I'm the one who'll get stuck taking care of it.'"

She smiled. "I always wanted a real cat, but my mother would never let me have one." Her smile faded. "Would you rather have a dog?"

He grinned. "That's so 'you'—always thinking of someone else's needs and wants before your own." He shook his head. "Maybe someday after we have children, if you're home more, we'll talk about a dog. But right now, with our hectic schedules, a cat will be a much better pet."

She nodded, snuggling the kitten again. "You're right. Would you like to name her?"

"Me? No, she's yours. You do the honors."

She thought for a moment. "How about Lady Luck, since she's a Fortune now?"

Kane smiled, nodding. "Lady Luck she is. Maybe she'll bring us luck."

She certainly hoped so, she thought, remembering her conversation with his father. Somehow she had to explain to her husband that she had spoken with his father and was planning to meet him.

And she had a bad feeling it was going to take a lot more than luck to make him understand.

But as the evening wore on, she couldn't seem to find a good time to introduce the subject. They played with the kitten and made a quick trip to the store for cat food and supplies. By then it was time for bed.

Kane shut Lady in the bathroom while he made slow, devastating love to Allison, but later she fell asleep with the sound of a tiny motor purring right next to her ear as Lady curled up on her pillow.

And she never did manage to tell Kane about his father. Moments before her eyes closed, she drowsily swore to herself that she'd tell him first thing in the morning. But his beeper went off at 4:00 a.m., and he was called to the hospital.

And as she dressed for work with the kitten pouncing on the laces of her sturdy white sneakers, she said out loud, "I'll tell him tonight, after I've seen his father."

Lady Luck paused in her pursuit of the lace and looked up at Allison, cocking her head as if she'd like to have the words repeated.

"I will," she said to the kitten.

Allison spotted Lloyd Carter right away when she stepped into the diner. Kane actually resembled his father a bit, she thought, especially his eyes. It wasn't something she thought he'd be pleased to know. But he would be glad that he'd inherited that strong, arrogant Fortune bone structure and jaw instead of his father's weaker, softer look. Kane in a temper was something to behold; she couldn't imagine anyone ever being afraid of Lloyd.

He rose when she approached and courteously held her chair with the easy grace of a man who always treated women courteously. "Howdy," he said, taking her hand. "I appreciate you coming. Would you like something to eat? To drink?"

She took the offered seat. "Just some coffee, please."

The hovering waitress headed off to the counter and Lloyd took his own seat. The conversation was stilted and awkward, and she glanced at her watch, wishing she knew how to cut this short. But then Kane's father began to talk about what had occurred thirty years ago, and she forgot about leaving.

"I was a high-school drop-out," Lloyd told her. "I hit the rodeo circuit because I didn't know how to do anything but rope and ride, and I didn't want to work on a ranch. All cowboys dream of making it big in rodeo." He laughed and his eyes crinkled, his smile flashing. "Everybody thinks it's glamorous."

Lloyd had charming moments, she had to admit. If he was younger, and if she didn't know what she knew about him, she'd probably have said he was attractive.

"It's not glamorous." His smile faded. "It's dusty and dirty and you live with bruises and broken bones and dis-locations—and that's the lucky ones. There's next to no money in it unless you're one of the big names."

He looked down at the table. "I did pretty decent for a while. Made a living. That's when I met Randi." He shook his head and his eyes were far away. "She was the prettiest thing I'd ever seen. She came to a rodeo and once I caught sight of her, that was that. She used to have long hair like yours, only a little more yellow in it."

"So you two got married."

Lloyd nodded. "She'd just given up the twins, which she didn't tell me right away. But she was always a little sad, a little down when she thought no one was looking and I finally got it out of her. I just wanted to make her happy again. So we got married and she started traveling right along with me." He shook his head. "When I think of the way we lived…and what she must have been used to…''

''So she traveled around with you.'' She wanted to get him back on track.

''Yeah. For a while we did okay. And then she got pregnant.'' His fingers drummed a nervous tattoo on the table. ''I'd just had a real bad ride and got my right knee torn up pretty bad, so I couldn't work. We were in California, so that's where we stayed. She got a job working tables at a pancake joint until the boy was born and afterward she went right back to it.''

''What did she do with Kane while she worked?''

''I took care of him.'' Pride flashed across Lloyd's face, and Allison sat back, bemused. ''He was a good little fella. I carried him around to stock auctions and such with me. My knee was about patched up, and I was ready to get back on the circuit. But then Randi got pregnant again.''

Allison's eyebrows rose. ''All by herself,'' she said dryly.

Lloyd had the grace to flush. ''She changed after that,'' he said sadly. ''She wanted me to get a job, but she wasn't happy when I talked about rodeoing again. She wanted to settle down. We fought all the time. She finally told me she didn't need me and that I could just get out…'' he paused, then said sadly ''…and she didn't, either. She did just fine without me.''

He clasped his hands together, and Allison saw that his fingers were shaking. Pity crept in around the edges of her exasperation.

''So I left,'' he said quietly. ''I'm not proud of it. I just left. Always meant to go back, though.'' His tone was defensive. ''But a year sneaked by, and then another, and by the time I got back to my family, Randi was gone. I never even knew if the second one was a girl or boy until I got that letter from Gabrielle.''

''And that's when you found out Miranda was one of the Fortunes.''

He nodded. ''Shouldn't have surprised me like it did. I used to call her my princess because of her manners and the way she talked, like she'd had a real expensive education.''

''If you wanted to reunite with your children again, why did you blackmail Miranda?'' Allison asked quietly. ''Surely you realized that Kane and Gabrielle wouldn't think highly of that.''

Lloyd shook his head. ''That wasn't my idea,'' he said. ''Like a dumb cowboy, I told Leeza about Randi's twin babies a year or so ago, and she got the bright idea to hunt them up.''

She thought briefly of pointing out that he could have refused, but it would have been an exercise in futility. There just wasn't that kind of backbone in this man. Even if he'd stayed with Miranda, she couldn't imagine that the marriage would have lasted. Miranda was vibrant and strong-willed—she would need an equally strong man to balance her.

''Thank you for telling me this,'' she said. ''I can't promise you anything—''

''But I know you'll try.'' Lloyd's bright smile was back. He seemed to have an optimistic ability to ignore reality when it didn't suit him…and apparently always had.

She rose, glancing at her watch. ''I really need to go.''

''Thanks again for letting me explain it,'' he said, rising. ''If I could just make Kane understand…''

She nodded without speaking further, and slipped away from the table. As she left the diner she glanced back through the window. Kane's father was sitting alone in the corner, staring into his coffee cup. His face looked so sad that she had to fight the urge to turn around and go back inside.

He only wanted to get home. Kane sighed as he turned into the gated community that included his mother's house. He might have begged off with some excuse but his mother rarely bothered him at the hospital, and she'd sounded upset when they'd spoken. After being called out before dawn, he hadn't gotten home again until after Allison had left for work. He'd slept for a few hours and then gone back to the hospital for his regular rounds. He'd had to deal with yet another crisis, and Allison's shift had ended by the time he'd gotten free.

He strode into the house without knocking, noting that his uncle Ryan's car was parked ahead of his in the circle. "Mother? Emma? I'm here."

"Kane." Emma came out of the study, walking toward him with a smile on her face. Her resemblance to his mother startled him a little bit each time they met, but he was getting used to the similarities. There were differences, too. After all, his mother wasn't expecting a baby.

Emma positively glowed with good health. In his chosen field, he usually saw post-birth mothers with tear-stained faces and overlarge clothing hovering anxiously, waiting for him to tell them their babies would make it. So his half sister, with her smiling blue eyes and round little tummy, was a welcome sight. What would Allison look like when her belly was swollen with his child?

The thought pleased him. A lot. Maybe they should stop worrying about contraception and just take their chances.

He took Emma's outstretched hands and held them wide before planting a kiss on her cheek. "If every pregnant woman looked like you, women would want to be pregnant," he said, grinning.

"Thanks." Her face lit up even more. "If I had any money, I'd pay you to follow me around and say things like that." She pointed toward the study. "Miranda and Ryan are in the study. Why don't you come in?"

"What's wrong?"

Emma's smile faded. "I think I'd better let them explain."

She hadn't gained a lot of weight, he observed with a critical medical eye as he followed her down the hall. The only weight she seemed to have gained was all baby. From the back, he couldn't even tell she was pregnant.

He'd gotten to know Emma a bit better each time he'd seen her. She was cheerful and friendly, one of those people whose glass was half-full no matter how difficult her life. And it had been difficult, he suspected. She was quite good at evading questions about herself.

The study door was ajar, and he followed her into the room. His mother was seated in a wing chair and Ryan was pacing back and forth in front of the small gas fireplace. The atmosphere—tension and shock mingled with a healthy dose of anger—hit him full in the face and instinctively he braced himself for bad news.

"Mother," he said cautiously by way of greeting as he bent to kiss her. "Ryan." He nodded to his uncle. "What's going on?"

"You'll never believe it." His uncle's face was as weary as he'd ever seen it.

Kane ignored the advice, spearing his uncle with a glance. "Tell me."

"Your father and his charming wife have been busy little bees." There was an uncharacteristic note of bitterness in Miranda's voice. "They hired Flynn Sinclair—remember him?—to check into your uncle Cameron's background. Don't ask me how, but they've located three people they say are illegitimate offspring of Cam's.''

"It's entirely believable," Ryan put in. "Cameron was...less than faithful to his wife."

Cameron Fortune, Ryan and Miranda's eldest brother, had died in a scandalous accident in which his young assistant, supposedly his latest lover, had also been killed before Kane had come to San Antonio. According to the papers, Cameron had had a string of extracurricular ladies in his life for years. Ryan was right—it was believable.

"Let me guess," he said, anger beginning to boil beneath the surface. "My dear old dad wants a 'small sum' of money before he gives you particulars."

"We've already paid him," Miranda said tonelessly. "Twenty-five grand. We have the names and addresses of these people, and Flynn is waiting to hear from us. He'll inform them of their heritage if we want him to, much as he did for Emma and Justin."

"If you're going to pursue it, he's the man for the job," Emma offered. "If there's any way to tell someone that you know who their biological family is, he's got it down pat."

"How do you know Carter isn't just making this up?" demanded Kane. "These people could be anybody. Only DNA work will prove his claims."

"You're forgetting the birthmark." Miranda pointed at Emma, Ryan and finally at Kane himself as she spoke. "Every single member of our family that I know of has that crown-shaped birthmark on the hip." She held up a sheaf of papers that had been lying in her lap. "Flynn's done a lot of legwork already. I don't even want to know how he got his hands on some of these hospital records, but they show that each of these three has the mark."

"Damn." Kane sat down abruptly.

"Yeah," said Ryan. "Exactly." He shook his head, trying to smile. "I've been cleaning up after Cameron my whole life. I guess it was too much to hope that there weren't any messes left to be fixed."

"Look on the bright side," said Emma. "You'll be gaining three new family members."

"You're right." Miranda stood decisively. "Why wouldn't we welcome them just as we welcomed you? It doesn't make any difference how we learned about them." Her eyes narrowed. "But I'm not finished with Lloyd. If he's got any more surprises for us, I'm going to know about them."

"So we're agreed that we should send Sinclair to approach these people?" Ryan looked at Kane. "Until we get a response from him, maybe we shouldn't say anything to the rest of the family."

Kane nodded. "Probably wise."

"I know." Miranda snapped her fingers. "Let's plan a family reunion. You can host it at the Double Crown, Ryan. We'll tell everyone we want to introduce the newest members of the family, meaning Emma and Justin. And Allison also hasn't met most of them, come to think of it. We can invite these new children of Cam's and if they agree, we can introduce them then as well."

"Yeah," said Kane, his voice heavy with sarcasm. "And that way we can also invite any more family members my loving father uncovers between now and then."

"I doubt there are more," said Ryan quietly. "I'm frankly stunned that Cameron fathered three children in addition to his own three. Mary Ellen is going to be shattered," he added, referring to Cameron's widow, who had since remarried in a ceremony Kane had attended several years ago.

Privately, Kane doubted Mary Ellen would be "shattered." The whole family knew of Cameron's philandering ways; even his own children acknowledged that their father had been flawed.

A deep, burning rage festered within him, fueled by a healthy dose of humiliation. His father was the one who had created all these problems. Though he could honestly say he was glad to be getting to know Emma, he could never forget or forgive the fact that his mother had been blackmailed by his father. And now the man was spreading his poison again. Helped, no doubt, by that pluperfect bitch of a bleached blonde he called a wife. No, he corrected, probably directed by her.

"So," said Emma, "what do you know about these new relations?"

Miranda looked down over the sheaf of papers. "Two men and a woman," she reported. "The eldest, Samuel Pearce, is a Marine and he was born...the year that Cam married Mary Ellen!" Her voice was outraged. With a visible effort, she calmed herself and read further. "Jonas Goodfellow is three years younger than Samuel and lives in San Francisco. He's involved in international imports. The girl—the woman," she corrected herself, "is a good bit younger. Holly Douglas is Gabrielle's age. And she's originally from Texas but now she lives in... Good grief! Alaska. It says she owns and runs a general store in a small town."

Ryan picked up the phone on Miranda's desk. "I'll try to get hold of Sinclair. He's going to be logging some serious flying time this week."

Nine

Kane drove home in the filthiest mood he could remember in years. Rage alternately simmered below the surface and erupted repeatedly, and he snarled as he slammed the Explorer to a halt in his own driveway. God, he wished he'd never heard the name *Carter,* much less used it for over two decades. The man was scum. How could he sell relatives, blood relationships, as if they had a fixed value beyond which they didn't matter?

Easily, he realized. After all, his own blood relationships had nothing to him in his own life until they'd acquired a monetary value. He'd seen through his father's pathetic attempt at claiming kinship the very first time he'd laid eyes on the man. He and Gabrielle now were worth cultivating because they were Fortunes.

It was growing dark as he disarmed the security system and went into the house, resetting it behind him. "Allison?" He needed her.

His wife came down the hallway. She wore a sheer blue peignoir with a matching short silk robe that showed off long slender legs. "Welcome home." She carried a glass of wine in her hand and she offered it to him as she reached him. "I feel like I haven't seen you in ages."

He took the wine from her without saying a word and set it down on the hall table, pulling her into his arms in the same motion. "I need you," he muttered, covering her mouth.

As her eyes drifted closed, he saw the stunned pleasure lighting them and he knew why. He'd never admitted anything like that to her before. "Tell me you love me," he whispered against her lips.

"I love you." It was a husky purr. "I love you."

He kissed his way down her throat, frantically devouring her soft white flesh as he gripped her slender body and locked her against him. She smelled fresh and sweet and her skin was damp, as if she'd just come from the shower. "Let's go upstairs." He lifted her into his arms; although she always protested, he liked carrying her.

But tonight she didn't protest. As she put her arms around his neck, she said, "We don't have to go upstairs. There are rooms down here we haven't christened yet."

Her words jolted his burgeoning desire and instead of heading for the stairs he turned left into the kitchen. "You're right." He set her on the edge of the kitchen counter with her legs on either side of his hips and opened his pants quickly, groaning when she reached between them to free him. Her hands on him made his blood boil and he pushed himself more firmly into her grasp as his big palms stroked up her thighs, pushing high the skimpy fabric of her lingerie. To his delight, he discovered she wasn't wearing any panties beneath the blue silk.

Tearing himself away from her, he knelt before her and

gently pressed his mouth against the mound of soft blond curls between her legs. She moaned and moved restlessly against him. Slowly, he used his tongue to stroke a light path along her feminine folds, opening her to him a little more with each stroke. She tasted spicy and female; when he glanced up at her, she had propped her weight back on her palms and her head was thrown back. Her hips rose and fell. When he sucked lightly at the small hidden bud he'd found, she gave a strangled scream, and her body arched wildly.

He wanted to see her climax, but he was selfish, too. He wanted to be inside her when she came. The mere thought was almost too erotic to bear. Quickly he rose and positioned himself at her small opening.

Then, pausing, he swore. "I'm not using anything."

"No," she agreed, smiling like a satisfied cat, her green eyes mere slits, "you certainly aren't." She pushed her hips forward, capturing just the tip of him and he groaned, trying desperately to focus.

"Shall I stop?"

"No." She put her hands at his hips to hold him to her.

"Would you mind if we made a baby tonight?" It was a rough growl.

"I wouldn't mind." She wrapped her hand around him and began to stroke his hardened flesh. "I want to have your baby."

Her small fingers caressing him made him grit his teeth against the wild surge of his body, but he couldn't bring himself to make her stop. "And I want you to have my babies," he managed. "Whenever it happens, it happens."

He wrapped his hands around her and held her steady for his first deep thrust, then found a fast, furious rhythm, pounding into her as she clung to his body. Her hands drifted down his back and palmed his buttocks and as her climax approached, she held him tightly to her, fingers digging deep into the sensitive crevice.

They were both panting and winded. He dropped his head to her shoulder for a moment, but his legs were shaking. Giggling, she held his opened pants around his waist as he staggered into the living room and half fell onto the couch, rolling her beneath him. He loved her so much, this small, quiet woman who'd never asked him for anything, who'd been happy to come be his wife and live with him and make his life better than anything he'd ever known.

Then he realized what he'd just admitted to himself. He loved her! Of course he loved her. He'd been fighting it for a while, losing the battle degree by degree.

Dropping his forehead to hers, he kissed her gently. They both were still breathing heavily, and he smiled. As soon as he caught his breath, he was going to tell her.

"Where's the kitten?" he asked.

She smiled. "Upstairs, sleeping on my pillow."

"Good." He kissed her again. "It might have done her permanent psychological damage if she'd seen what we just did."

The telephone on the end table rang at that moment. They both jumped a little; it was right behind their heads.

Kane grinned. "You'd better answer that. The way I'm breathing, people will know exactly what we've been up to." Reaching over her head, he punched the button for the speaker.

"Fortune residence, Allison speaking." She smiled up at him as she spoke.

"Howdy, Allison." A jovial masculine voice filled the room, and her body stiffened in horror as she recognized it. "I just wanted to say thanks and tell you it was nice to get together with you the other afternoon. I know you'll do

everything you can to make Kane see the truth. It's Lloyd,''
the man added belatedly.

Allison's body had gone rigid beneath Kane's at the very
first word. Through the rage that rushed in to fill every
corner of his brain like an inexorable tide, Kane realized
she'd known who it was right away. He stared down at her
with dry, burning eyes and watched her face go dead white,
then immediately flush a dark, damning red.

"I—uh—"

"I'd like to meet again one of these days. Next time I'll
do the listening.'' His father chuckled, then said again,
"Well, ah, thanks. You're the best hope I have of reuniting
with my son and—"

"No, Carter, she's not.'' Kane's voice was cold and furious as he levered himself off her and stood in one lithe
motion. "There is *no hope* that you and I will ever even
occupy the same building again, much less reunite. Now
leave my wife the hell alone and don't *ever* try to contact
either one of us again.''

"Kane?'' Carter's voice sounded shocked, uncertain.
"Kane, I—"

In one sudden, violent move, he slammed down the receiver and stared at his wife.

With trembling fingers, Allison drew the blanket from
the back of the couch and covered herself with it. Her eyes
were huge and her face drained of color again as she stared
back.

"Damn you,'' he said hoarsely. "How long have you
been going behind my back, meeting him?''

"Only once.'' Her voice was small. She clearly knew
she'd been wrong. His rage grew. He'd trusted her. Even
when he'd married her, some part of him had known he
could trust her implicitly. He'd come to depend on her, to

need her, to believe in her ability to make his life happy. He'd been going to tell her he *loved* her!

"He called twice before. The first time he wanted to talk to you. The second time he—"

"I don't care about the second time." He turned away from her, too upset and furious even to look at her. He fastened his pants as he spoke. "You knew what I think of him. You knew I didn't want him to have anything to do with my family. *You knew!*" It was a roar of rage. "I trusted you and you went sneaking around behind my back to meet a man who's managed to upset my entire family."

Allison's face was even whiter. "You give him too much importance. And look what the end result was. Even if he went about it for selfish reasons, you still got Emma and Justin."

"And I'm about to get three new cousins," he snarled.

At the uncomprehending look on her face, he sneered. "Oh, did he neglect to mention that to you? My loving father has discovered three illegitimate kids of my uncle Cameron's and *for a small fee,* he was kind enough to share the information with us."

"When—how—" she stammered.

"My mother called me today," he said. "I stopped by on the way home. That—that *slug*—is ruining my whole family!" It was an exaggeration, of course, but in some ways that was how it felt. The fragile status quo he'd finally learned to accept would be tilted wildly off-balance once again. The Fortune clan was nothing if not volatile; he could only imagine some of his cousins' reactions to Lloyd's demands.

"Kane, I know he's got flaws." She twisted her fingers in the blanket. "But I believe he's sincere about wanting to get to know you—"

"Hell, yes, he's sincere," he shouted, goaded beyond

restraint. "I'm a Fortune now. That surely gives me some worth in his eyes. Maybe if he gets on my good side I'll let him sponge off my family's wealth." He wheeled and stomped back into the kitchen, "I want nothing to do with him and *you knew it!*"

"I knew it." She had followed him into the kitchen. "But I thought you were wrong. I still do." Her voice shook, but she kept it level with an obvious effort.

It was a shock to have her challenge him. He was used to thinking of Allison as a soothing presence, a peacemaker, an oasis of calm. If she'd ever seriously disagreed with him before he couldn't remember it. For the first time he realized there was a core of steel beneath his wife's gentle exterior. Not readily evident nor used for harm, perhaps, but she wouldn't bend and break as easily as he'd always assumed. The realization only made him angrier. "I don't care what you think," he said brutally.

But she went on, in that same level, inflexible tone. "You loathe the man. You won't give him the time of day much less a chance to talk to you."

"He *had* a chance," Kane shouted. "But he was too damned busy blackmailing my family! And encouraging my own wife to lie to me."

"I have never lied to you!" Her tone was vehement.

"Not in words, maybe. But a lie of omission is still a lie. For all I know, you're helping him with his filthy little schemes."

She gasped and he could see her recoil at the words. "That's ridiculous."

"Is it?" Of course it was, but he knew it would hurt her. And he *wanted* her to hurt, damn her! He wanted her to feel the way he felt when he'd realized what she'd done. "What else haven't you told me about his plans for my family?"

"He *is* part of your family." Her eyes were dark with pain but her voice was steady. "Someday it will be too late for you ever to talk to him again. And I feel sorry for you, Kane, if you let the past keep you from making that connection. I missed that chance with my father and I'll regret it until the day I die."

He couldn't look at her; he was too mad. Instead he stared through the glass of the French doors at the still waters of the moonlit pool, hands clenched at his hips. "I will *never* forgive you for this."

An hour later, Kane rested himself on the edge of the pool with his elbows.

The horrible shock of hearing his father talking to Allison had faded. Now what he remembered most vividly were his own harsh words and the shattered look on her face.

He hadn't been looking at her when he'd said the nastiest of the hateful words he'd hurled at her: *I will never forgive you for this.* But he'd heard her shocked intake of breath, as if he'd slapped her. And then she'd slipped from the kitchen, and he'd heard her moving up the stairs. That was when he'd torn open the door and stormed outside.

Now, physically spent from the vigorous exercise, his rage expended on plowing through the water like a madman, he just felt...empty.

And guilty. Okay, so he'd been mad at Allison for talking to his father. He knew her well enough to understand that she would have been fundamentally unable to refuse a plea if she perceived it as honest. And he generally considered her an excellent judge of character.

I missed that chance with my father and I'll regret it until the day I die.

Oh, God. Could she be right? He didn't know. Right now

he didn't think there was an ounce of compassion in him to extend to Lloyd. But still...

Far more important, he had to patch things up with her. He rarely let his temper slip its leash because he always regretted it, and this occasion was no exception. His anger had blinded him momentarily and he'd behaved inexcusably. Allison would never conspire against him. She loved him. He groaned and rested his head against the tiles of the poolside. What could he say that would erase the hurt he'd inflicted?

Very little, he realized as he pulled himself from the pool, grabbed his discarded clothes and headed for the house. All he could do was beg her to forgive him.

A few minutes later, he opened the door to the garage and his heart sank. Her car was gone.

He'd headed straight upstairs to talk to her but she hadn't been there. And when he'd glanced through the master suite, he'd seen little signs that bothered him, missing items, toiletries, her hairbrush, the romance novel she'd been reading that had been on her bedside table. Only the kitten had been left, still sleeping peacefully on the bed. And that was when the first stirrings of panic had struck.

Now they had coalesced into a full-fledged storm inside him. She'd left him. Dear God, he'd never imagined that she would leave. They'd had a *fight;* that was all. But clearly it had been more than that to her.

She must have left while he was swimming. His own splashing would have masked the sound of the Mazda's engine starting or the garage door moving up and down.

He'd been going to tell her he loved her, he remembered suddenly. She didn't even have that to comfort her. No wonder she'd thought he didn't want her anymore.

I will never forgive you for this. Another fresh arrow of guilt quivered through him as he thought of what those

words must have meant to her. He knew how her life had
changed after her father had left. He could imagine living
with someone as depressed as her mother must have been,
could see how mental illness had leached beauty and vi-
tality from her mother. And he knew Allison had seen it
as well.

She hid herself behind a bland exterior because she'd
seen how little external beauty really meant...how little it
had meant in her own parents' lives. And she'd hidden her
own natural loveliness for years, avoiding even the chance
at a relationship that could destroy her as her mother had
been destroyed.

But he'd seen through her. She was beautiful all the way
through, and he'd been amazingly lucky to have realized it
and to have married her before someone else recognized
what a treasure she was.

But to her, even marriage didn't guarantee a lifetime of
commitment. She'd grown up believing that marriages
didn't last forever. To her ears, his hastily uttered words
probably had sounded like the death knell of a marriage.
She must have been convinced that he was ending theirs.

His hand shook as he reached for the telephone. First he
called the hospital. After an interminable wait, he'd been
informed that she wasn't working at this time. Next, he
dialed his sister. Gabrielle had taken Allison to lunch once
or twice and they'd been becoming friends; maybe she'd
gone to her.

But Gabrielle, with distinct concern in her voice, reported that she hadn't seen or heard from Allison.

The next call he placed was to his mother's house. God,
he hated to confess what he'd done, but that didn't matter
as long as Allison came home. All his life he'd worked to
be perfect, to excel at whatever he chose to pursue. But his

pride would be a cold companion if he couldn't make Allison see that he hadn't meant to drive her away.

When Miranda answered, he rushed into speech before she could respond. "Lloyd asked Allison to help him effect some kind of peace with me. When I found out...I didn't take it very well. Given that she knew how I felt about him, it didn't make any sense to me that she would do that."

"It makes perfect sense to me," his mother said tartly. "Allison is a peacemaker, Kane. You know that. She must feel strongly about this, because I know for a fact that girl lives and breathes to make you happy."

"She and her father were estranged," he admitted. "And he died before she could forgive him. She didn't want me to have the same regrets she does."

There was a momentary silence. Then his mother said quietly, "She really loves you, Kane."

He winced, feeling panic rise anew at the memory of his hasty words. "I told her he didn't mean it," he confessed. "I accused him of only wanting to get close to me because of my family connections."

On the other end of the line, his mother sighed. "For what it's worth, he might be sincere. Lloyd seems genuinely sorry that he let so many years go by. At least," she urged, "hear him out."

"I'm not sure I can do that." He might as well be honest. "How could he blackmail you like he has if he has even a shred of decency?"

His mother hesitated. "Lloyd...was a kind, decent man when we were married, Kane. Regardless of what happened afterward, he was very good to me at the lowest point in my life. I wasn't the woman I am now when I met him. I was a scared, unhappy teenager who needed someone to lean on. It wasn't until I began to regain my self-confidence and assert myself that things changed." Miranda made a sound of distaste. "You didn't meet the Lloyd I knew that day when he came here. He appears to be—" she hesitated again, as if choosing her words with care "—very much under the influence of his current spouse."

"You can say that again." Just the memory of that woman made his skin crawl. The thought struck him that living with her every day had to be a kind of punishment in itself. That marriage couldn't be anything like his and Allison's, and he almost—almost—felt a twinge of pity for Lloyd Carter.

Still…having a heart-to-heart with his father wasn't high on his list right now. After he'd asked Miranda to call immediately if anyone in the family heard from Allison, another thought occurred to him. There were a lot of things he'd rather do, but…

Reluctantly, he pulled out his wallet and extracted a torn slip of paper. His father's phone number. He'd taken it from his mother's desk after that first meeting because he'd been afraid they might have to track the man down again. Now, he just prayed his father hadn't moved.

"Hello?"

"Carter? It's Kane Fortune." He closed his eyes against the conflicting emotions that blasted through him.

"Kane? I'm glad you called back." His father's voice was notably subdued. "I hope I didn't cause any trouble between you and Allison. She's one special lady."

"Yes, she is." Kane cleared his throat. "Um, you haven't seen her, have you?"

Dead silence. "Ah, hell. This is all my fault." Dejection and self-directed rage sounded over the connection. "No, I'm sorry to tell you I haven't seen her. I'll let you know if I do."

"Thanks." He didn't know what else to say.

"Kane…I'm sorry for butting into your life, for trying

to force you to accept me.'' His father took a deep breath. ''I promise you I won't do it again. And I'll never come asking for money again, either.''

''I want to believe that.'' It was the best he could do. He hesitated, then said, ''Maybe I'll call you again someday.'' Though he didn't know if he'd ever be able to forgive the man's abandonment, he knew that because it meant so much to Allison, he'd try.

''That'd be great.'' Lloyd sounded so pathetically hopeful that Kane winced. ''Now go find your gal.''

Problem was, he didn't have a clue where to go looking. She hadn't contacted any of their—his—family. She wasn't at the hospital. If she had close female friends, he'd never heard about them.

Then again, he thought, he hadn't exactly encouraged her confidences during their short marriage. He'd spent half of their relationship resenting the hell out of his need for her and the other half in bed with her. The few times they'd had long opportunities to talk, he'd been the one doing most of the yakking. She had a way of deflecting attention and making him want to share things with her that tended to obscure the fact that she wasn't doing much sharing in return.

Not with her past, anyway. In every other respect, Allison had been willing to share anything with him. He slumped onto the barstool at the counter and stared at the receiver he'd replaced. Where was she, and when would she call him?

She wouldn't call Kane if somebody were driving needles into her feet, Allison thought the next day, looking around the depressing little living room. Several times during the interminably long night she'd nearly given in to the urge to call him, just to hear his beloved voice.

But she wouldn't. She couldn't. Her marriage had been a mistake, a sham into which she'd been the only one pouring love and affection and energy—

Not strictly true, her conscience reminded her. Kane had been openly affectionate in the past few weeks and had seemed to need her in the same way she needed him. But need and love were two different things. And she couldn't live with him without love.

She didn't know when she'd had that revelation, but it was true. She loved him so much that she'd do almost anything for him. But she needed his love in return. She *deserved* his love. Her mother had never believed that of herself; after her husband's rejection and departure she had simply folded in on herself, leading a quiet, joyless existence centered around Allison. She'd been an attractive woman of forty when her husband had left her, but she'd seemed decades older after that.

It had been one heck of a role model. Easy to see now. She'd feared rejection so much that she'd almost missed the chance to marry and share her love and her life with someone. Loving Kane, living with him, had been wonderful. It had changed her life in some very good ways, But ever since she'd confessed her love for him, she'd felt something was missing—and she knew what it was. She needed to hear the words.

She'd hoped against hope that someday he would return those words, and for a while it had seemed as if he eventually might. And that had been all right with her. She'd been willing to wait.

But his reaction yesterday had showed her just how flimsy the foundations of her hope had been. Kane didn't love her. He'd never loved her. And the naked rage in his voice when he'd said, "I'll never forgive you for this," had convinced her that he never would. Forgive *or* love.

And so she'd left. She'd start over again somewhere, alone. But this time she wouldn't expect to find love. Twice now she'd seen what love did to people and she didn't intend to ever feel like this again.

But maybe someday, when the hurt wasn't so sharp and fierce it felt as though her heart had been torn from her chest, she'd look for friendship and the kind of companionship she could share for the rest of her life. She might not have love, but her marriage to Kane had shown her that she didn't want to live the rest of her life alone. She wanted a family. Someone to laugh with, to share the small intimacies of daily life. Children of her own to cuddle and nurture.

"Miss Preston?" She'd given the apartment manager her maiden name since she expected she'd soon be taking it back.

"This is fine," she said dully, handing the woman a check for the deposit and a month's rent. It was a by-the-month lease, hard to find but perfect for her right now until she decided what she was going to do, where she was going to go.

Where to go. She was leaving San Antonio, of that she was sure. She had no family, no ties to the city, nothing to keep her here. With a pang, she thought of Miranda, of Emma and Gabrielle and Ryan and Lily—*Kane's family,* she reminded herself. *Not yours.*

So she was getting out of town. There was no way she could live here where Fortunes were daily headlines, no way she could work at County General and bump into Kane in the nurses' station and the halls. The thought brought the ever-ready tears to the surface. No, she didn't want to see Kane ever again.

Ten

It was no trouble settling into the tiny, furnished studio apartment. Allison had brought very little with her. She was off for the next two days and she spent part of her time at the public library on the Internet, looking at hospitals and locations, trying to decide where she might like to settle.

On the third day, after another sleepless night, she dressed and drove to the hospital.

Her nerves were frayed and about to get worse. Would she see Kane? What would he do? Say? Maybe nothing. He'd be glad she'd left, she was sure.

She'd just put away her things and was walking toward the desk when he stepped out of the elevator. He looked both ways and when he saw her, a grim smile touched his mouth. "Wife."

She didn't trust herself not to sob as a wave of fresh grief tore through her. He looked a little tired—maybe he'd had a late night—but to her eyes, as wonderful as always.

"Where have you been?" He'd stopped directly in front of her. His eyes were fierce, his tone aggressive.

She hesitated a moment. "I found a place to live," she said neutrally, forcing calm into her voice.

"You already have a place to live, in case you'd forgotten." He lowered his voice as a licensed practical nurse walked by. "We need to talk."

She shook her head, avoiding those intense eyes, struggling to keep her composure. "Not right now."

"When?"

"Dr. Fortune to the E.R., Dr. Fortune to the E.R." The loudspeaker blared right next to Allison's head, and she jumped, startled.

"Damn!" He checked his pager. "I've got to go. Do not leave this hospital without me today unless you're going home."

She only stared at him. *Going home?*

The nursing supervisor rushed down the hallway, interrupting the tense moment. "Go to the E.R. with Dr. Fortune," she said, pointing to Allison. "I'll be sending isolettes and some other things down right away—we have a mom carrying triplets coming in with premature labor and bleeding."

Allison's eyed widened as her nurse's training took over. Personal problems took a back seat to helping save lives. Without another word she turned and headed for the elevator, but Kane touched her arm and pointed to the lighted exit sign. "The stairs would be faster."

She nodded, following him to the stairwell and they rushed down the steps, running headlong the rest of the way to the E.R. The woman was being brought in on a gurney as they donned gowns and masks, and within minutes the atmosphere was a tense mixture of professional directions and observations.

The obstetrician had arrived only moments before they had. When serious signs of fetal distress were detected, he took the unusual step of doing an emergency Caesarian section right there in the emergency room's operating area. Allison's heart sank when she heard that the babies were only twenty-seven weeks' gestation. Staff from all over the hospital descended with additional supplies and equipment as the babies were delivered: a very small boy who wasn't breathing, a slightly larger girl who was, and another girl even smaller than the boy, also in respiratory distress. Kane took charge of the baby boy and supervised two additional pediatricians who worked on the girls as they inserted catheters and needles and tubes and monitored vital signs. The biggest girl was stabilized and taken to the peds neonatal unit, but the other two continued to present challenge after challenge as they transferred them.

The smallest girl was stabilized two hours after delivery, but her condition was poor and there was nothing they could do but watch and wait. Allison could see the concern in Kane's eyes, but he continued to work to save the baby boy. Three hours later, the child was as stable as he could be, given his condition. Kane's face was grim and exhausted as he headed for a shower, and Allison watched the defeated set of his shoulders as he strode down the hall to talk to the parents first. She knew he expected that at least one of the preemies might not make it.

Allison slipped away to her locker, washed, gathered her things, totally drained. No one could have fought harder for those babies, she thought fiercely. No one. Her chest ached from the effort of suppressing sobs.

She went to the personnel office as soon as she'd cleaned up. Today had been overwhelmingly awful, and not just because they'd nearly lost two of the three babies. Today had shown her that she couldn't work with Kane, day in and day out. It would kill her to be in such close proximity to him, to feel his pain and not be able to soothe or comfort him.

The personnel director seemed surprised when she asked if there were any openings into which she could transfer. One of the nurses in the pediatric oncology unit was going on maternity leave starting Monday, and though it would be a temporary position, it suited her purposes. In six weeks, chances were good that she'd have found work elsewhere and she'd be leaving San Antonio anyway.

After thanking the personnel director, she walked out to her car, her footsteps dragging. The sun was low and it would soon be growing dark. Her spirits matched the darkening winter sky above.

Then she saw Kane leaning against her little red car and she slowed even more. He never looked up as she approached, merely slouched there with his hands in his jacket pockets, not moving a muscle, and no matter how slowly she moved, it was inevitable that she'd have to approach him eventually.

"Hello," she said softly.

"Hello." He still didn't look up. Exhaustion and defeat carved deep lines on his handsome features.

She knew him, knew how he must be feeling after the disastrous day, and she couldn't stop herself from stepping closer and laying her hand on his forearm. He might not want her as his wife, but they'd been friends once, able to share their feelings about the work they both loved and hated at times. And she loved him so much it broke her heart to see him hurting. "Are you okay?"

"No." He looked at her then, and the pain screaming in his golden eyes hit her like a slap. "No, I'm not okay. Two times today I had to walk into a room and tell those people that their children were critically ill, that even if they live they might have serious handicapping conditions. It was…hell. All I could think of was how I would feel if that was a child of ours.''

She stroked his arm beneath the rough fabric of his sleeve. ''It isn't—''

''You're going to say it isn't my fault.'' He moved restlessly, dislodging her hand. ''And you're right. But it *is* my fault that you left me.''

He stepped closer, reaching for her before she could evade him. ''I'm sorry. Please come home?''

''Kane, I—''

''Don't talk.'' He subdued her half-hearted struggles easily, pulling her to his chest and after another moment of resistance, she stopped fighting him. His arms were hard and strong around her, and as he pressed her head against his shoulder, she inhaled the faint scent of his aftershave mingled with the pure essence of Kane that she'd come to know so well. It was Heaven and at the same time it was Hell. How could she bear to give him up?

''I'm sorry,'' he said again. ''I shouldn't have said the things I said to you about my father.''

''You were right, though.'' She spoke to his chest. ''I had absolutely no business talking to him.''

''No, I wasn't right.'' His arms tightened. ''I called him back after I realized you'd gone. We had a…civil conversation.''

''I'm glad.'' Her voice was uneven; it was a struggle to control her emotions. Of all the things she'd expected, hearing that Kane had approached his father and spoken to him was at the bottom of the list. She inhaled deeply, taking in the familiar masculine scent one more time, and she felt as if her heart were breaking right into two pieces. His arms around her were strong and secure, his heart beating steadily beneath her ear. God help her, but she didn't *want* to leave.

"You didn't answer me."

"Hmm?"

"I asked you to come home."

Could she stay with him, loving him as she did? Knowing he didn't love her?

He drew back a fraction, tilting her face up so that he could see her expression. In his own eyes she was shocked to see a surprising vulnerability, and she realized with a shock that he was afraid she was going to refuse.

Could she stay with him, loving him as she did? Knowing he didn't love her? The answer was clear. She loved him. That was the bottom line. Whether or not he felt the same way, she could no sooner walk away from him than she could excise the love she felt for him from her heart. He might never love her, but she couldn't withhold anything from him that he needed, and he needed *her.*

She smiled against his shoulder, an immense wave of relief rolling through her. A current of sadness still flowed, but it was buried deep beneath the conviction that this was right for her, for *them.* "You didn't ask. It was a command."

"I'm asking now." He leaned back and slid his arms from around her, bringing his hands up to cup her face. "Allison, I love you. I should have told you before. Will you please come home with me?"

"I—I—" She faltered and fell silent. "What?"

"I love you," he said again. "I don't want to spend a night without you in my arms ever again." His gaze searched her face and the lines of tension that had eased sprang back into sharp focus. "I'll beg, if that's what it takes. It took me too long to admit to myself that I love you."

"You love me." She felt lightheaded and her knees wobbled; she gripped his wrists to keep from sinking to the asphalt.

"I love you," he said again, gazing into her eyes. "I was going to tell you before—before my father called. Afterward…you left and I thought I'd never get the chance again." He hesitated, searching her face. When he spoke again his voice was strangely tentative, with none of his usual self-assurance. "You said you loved me. Do you still feel that way?"

"Do I still…?" She shook her head as a giddy, heady sense of wonder filled her. *He loved her!* "You really don't get it, do you?"

"Get what?" He didn't release her but she felt his withdrawal and his face was wary.

"I have loved you since the first day you smiled at me, you—you blind man!" She grabbed fistfuls of his shirt and shook him, though it was like shaking concrete. "I've loved you when you were grumpy at work, when you were too distracted to remember my name, when you treated me like…like an old, comfortable shoe. Good old Allison, my friend." She rolled her eyes. "I dreamed about you for *years.*"

"Why didn't you ever tell me?" Kane wasn't smiling but there was a light in his eyes that hadn't been there moments ago.

"What was I going to say?" She spread her hands. "Here's that instrument you asked for, Dr. Fortune. And oh, by the way, I love you." Then she sobered. "I…didn't think you found me attractive."

He snorted. "How would I have known if I had? You worked damn hard to make sure nobody ever noticed you." He shook his head reminiscently. "I can still remember how I felt the day I came out here and saw you with your hair down for the first time."

Her eyebrows rose. "You noticed me then? How did you feel?" He pulled her closer, sliding his arms around her and tilting her back over his arm for his kiss.

Off-balance, she put her arms around his neck and hung on for dear life as he set his lips on hers, deftly parting them and searching out the sweet recesses of her mouth with his tongue. He kissed her deeply, letting her come up for air only when his chest was heaving with the effort it took to control himself.

"I was terrified you had left me for good," he whispered, putting his forehead against hers.

"I had." She sobered. "I thought I'd never mean to you what you do to me."

His lips brushed hers and once again he gathered her to him. "You are more to me than I can ever put into words." And he showed her, holding her against his hard body, his hands streaking over her soft curves, his mouth plundering hers, leaving her in no doubt of his intentions.

"Is this a free show?" The amused feminine voice came from the same nurse who'd interrupted them in the lounge weeks ago.

And just as she had before, Allison tried to pull herself free of Kane's arms, only to find he had no intention of letting her go.

"Y'all better get on home where you can do that in private," the grinning woman advised. "Or we're going to be reading about certain members of the Fortune family arrested for indecent exposure."

"Or something like that," Kane said, laughing. He finally released Allison and took her hand, urging her across the parking lot to his vehicle. "Let's go home, wife. We'll get your car tomorrow."

"Maybe we could pick it up later today," she said.

But Kane shook his head as he put her into her seat, leaning in to kiss her deeply, drawing out the exchange until they both were breathing heavily again. "I have plans for the rest of today. And I guarantee they don't include picking up the car."

*   *   *   *   *

*Find out what happens when Flynn Sinclair
becomes Emma Michaels's
twenty-four hour protector*

in

THE PREGNANT HEIRESS,

*coming only to Silhouette Desire
in July 2001.*

*And now, for a sneak preview,
please turn the page.*

One

The party was being given by her uncle, Ryan Fortune, at his ranch outside the city. It was a big "welcome to the family" bash for her, her brother Justin, and two other Fortune relatives, cousins that the family had recently discovered, thanks to the efforts of Flynn Sinclair.

That man sure got around. He'd made his way into Emma's thoughts far too often in the past three weeks. But he'd been the catalyst for some important events in her life. It was no wonder she kept remembering that deep, laconic voice.

Elmo—or maybe Abigail—gave her a hard kick in the ribs in rebuttal.

Okay, so maybe she thought of Flynn a little too often. But there was no harm in a fantasy or two. She wasn't really interested in the man, no matter what effect he'd had on her unruly hormones. He was a P.I., for heavens sake. One step removed from a bounty hunter.

Like Steven.

Emma's shoulders tensed against the rush of fear. She had to stop reacting that way. It had been months since she'd fled San Diego in the dead of night, and Steven was very good at finding people who didn't want to be found. Surely, if he had been determined to track her down, he would have done it by now.

No, she wouldn't think about Steven. He was part of her past, not her present or her future. Better to think about all her new relatives. But would she ever feel as if these strangers were really family?

Probably not, she thought wistfully. She wasn't good at making permanent connections with people. But her baby would.

Well, she wasn't going to hang out in the hallway all night. She took a deep breath and plunged back into the crowd. She made it three feet before someone stopped her.

"There you are. I've been looking for you."

She knew that voice—deep, rumbly, as if each word rolled up from somewhere deep inside the big, broad chest of the man. She turned, her heartbeat picking up speed. "Flynn, I mean, Mr. Sinclair. I wondered if you would be here tonight."

He was too big. That was, once again, the first thing she noticed about the man—his size. Emma didn't like oversized men with tough-guy faces. Not even when they had superhero hair, black and shiny as wet Magic Marker, with an unruly curl that parted company with the rest of his hair to make an adorable little squiggle on his forehead.

"*Flynn* works fine." The corner of his mouth kicked up in the cocky grin she remembered. "I've been hoping I'd see you tonight."

He had? "Well—that's flattering." He couldn't have, she thought wryly, not when she was doing her seven-month impression of a blimp. "I was hoping to see you, too. I never thanked you."

His eyebrows lifted slightly. "No thanks needed. When I, ah, talked to you at the truck stop, I didn't get the impression that gratitude was one of your reactions."

"I was a little spooked at the time," she admitted. No need to tell him that she'd felt uneasy from the moment he'd sat down in her station. Flynn Sinclair simply did not have a reassuring face. His nose had been broken at least once; his eyes were set too deeply beneath thick black eyebrows.

And they were laughing at her right now. "I figured that out."

"You probably wondered why."

He shrugged those oversized shoulders. "I figured that out, too. You were running scared of someone—Steven Shaw. The man who got you pregnant. I've checked him out, and he's bad news."

"Tell me something I don't know! What right did you have to go digging around my personal life?" Had Flynn's meddling tipped Steven off?

"I'm a P.I." He wrapped one big hand around her arm. "How fixated is he on finding you?"

It was a frightening thought. "Steven used to talk to me about how he tracked people down, which has made finding a job rather difficult."

"A job? You're seven months pregnant. And you don't need money. Miranda Fortune is more than willing to take care of you, and the Lord knows she can afford it."

"I don't want or need to be taken care of!"

"Yeah, but you've got a baby to think of. I'd say you could use a little help."

How dare Flynn Sinclair imply that she couldn't take care of herself? Maybe she *had* to accept a little help right now. Nothing had changed, permanently, she assured herself. Steven would give up eventually. She'd get a job and a place of her own. She'd have her baby, and…

And then she wouldn't really be on her own anymore, would she?

Emma smiled and rubbed her stomach. Anita, or maybe Adam, was turning somersaults. No, she wouldn't be on her own anymore. She and her baby would be on *their* own— together.

FORTUNES OF TEXAS: THE LOST HEIRS
Fortune Family Tree

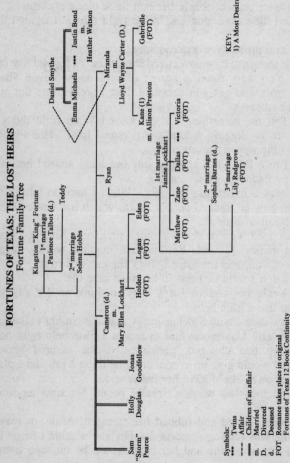

Kingston "King" Fortune

1st marriage — Patience Talbot (d.)
- Teddy

2nd marriage — Selena Hobbs

Cameron (d.)
m. Mary Ellen Lockhart

- Sam "Storm" Pearce
- Holly Douglas
- Jonas Goodfellow

- Holden (FOT)
- Logan (FOT)
- Eden (FOT)

Ryan

1st marriage — Janine Lockhart
- Matthew (FOT)
- Zane (FOT)
- Dallas (FOT)
- Victoria (FOT)

2nd marriage — Sophie Barnes (d.)

3rd marriage — Lily Redgrove (FOT)

Emma Michaels ••• Justin Bond
m.
Heather Watson

Daniel Smythe

Miranda
m.
Lloyd Wayne Carter (D.)
- Kane (1)
  m. Allison Preston
- Gabrielle (FOT)

KEY:
1) A Most Desirable M.D.

Symbols:
- ••• Twins
- – – Affair
- —— Children of an affair
- m. Married
- D. Divorced
- d. Deceased
- FOT Romance takes place in original Fortunes of Texas 12 Book Continuity

THE FORTUNES OF TEXAS

invite you to meet

THE LOST HEIRS

Silhouette Desire's scintillating
new miniseries, featuring the beloved

FORTUNES OF TEXAS

and six of your favorite authors.

A Most Desirable M.D.–June 2001
by Anne Marie Winston (SD #1371)

The Pregnant Heiress–July 2001
by Eileen Wilks (SD #1378)

Baby of Fortune–August 2001
by Shirley Rogers (SD #1384)

Fortune's Secret Daughter–September 2001
by Barbara McCauley (SD #1390)

Her Boss's Baby–October 2001
by Cathleen Galitz (SD #1396)

Did You Say Twins?!–December 2001
by Maureen Child (SD #1408)

And be sure to watch for *Gifts of Fortune*,
Silhouette's exciting new single title,
on sale November 2001

Don't miss these unforgettable romances…
available at your favorite retail outlet.

Silhouette®
Where love comes alive™

Feel like a star with Silhouette.

We will fly you and a guest to New York City for an exciting weekend stay at a glamorous 5-star hotel. Experience a refreshing day at one of New York's trendiest spas and have your photo taken by a professional. Plus, receive $1,000 U.S. spending money!

Flowers...long walks...dinner for two... how does Silhouette Books make romance come alive for you?

Send us a script, with 500 words or less, along with visuals (only drawings, magazine cutouts or photographs or combination thereof). Show us how Silhouette Makes Your Love Come Alive. Be creative and have fun. No purchase necessary. All entries must be clearly marked with your name, address and telephone number. All entries will become property of Silhouette and are not returnable. **Contest closes September 28, 2001.**

Please send your entry to: **Silhouette Makes You a Star!**

In U.S.A.	In Canada
P.O. Box 9069	P.O. Box 637
Buffalo, NY, 14269-9069	Fort Erie, ON, L2A 5X3

Look for contest details on the next page, by visiting www.eHarlequin.com or request a copy by sending a self-addressed envelope to the applicable address above. Contest open to Canadian and U.S. residents who are 18 or over. Void where prohibited.

Silhouette®
Where love comes alive™

Our lucky winner's photo will appear in a Silhouette ad. Join the fun!

HARLEQUIN "SILHOUETTE MAKES YOU A STAR!" CONTEST 1308
OFFICIAL RULES
NO PURCHASE NECESSARY TO ENTER

1. To enter, follow directions published in the offer to which you are responding. Contest begins June 1, 2001, and ends on September 28, 2001. Entries must be postmarked by September 28, 2001, and received by October 5, 2001. Enter by hand-printing (or typing) on an 8 ½" x 11" piece of paper your name, address (including zip code), contest number/name and attaching a script containing <u>500 words or less, along with drawings, photographs or magazine cutouts, or combinations thereof</u> (i.e., collage) <u>on no larger than 9" x 12"</u> piece of paper, describing how the <u>Silhouette books make romance come alive for you.</u> Mail via first-class mail to: Harlequin "Silhouette Makes You a Star!" Contest 1308, (in the U.S.) P.O. Box 9069, Buffalo, NY 14269-9069, (in Canada) P.O. Box 637, Fort Erie, Ontario, Canada L2A 5X3. Limit one entry per person, household or organization.

2. Contests will be judged by a panel of members of the Harlequin editorial, marketing and public relations staff. Fifty percent of criteria will be judged against script and fifty percent will be judged against drawing, photographs and/or magazine cutouts. Judging criteria will be based on the following:

   - Sincerity—25%
   - Originality and Creativity—50%
   - Emotionally Compelling—25%

   In the event of a tie, duplicate prizes will be awarded. Decisions of the judges are final.

3. All entries become the property of Torstar Corp. and may be used for future promotional purposes. Entries will not be returned. No responsibility is assumed for lost, late, illegible, incomplete, inaccurate, nondelivered or misdirected mail.

4. Contest open only to residents of the U.S. <u>(except Puerto Rico)</u> and Canada who are 18 years of age or older, and is void wherever prohibited by law; all applicable laws and regulations apply. Any litigation within the Province of Quebec respecting the conduct or organization of a publicity contest may be submitted to the Régie des alcools, des courses et des jeux for a ruling. Any litigation respecting the awarding of a prize may be submitted to the Régie des alcools, des courses et des jeux only for the purpose of helping the parties reach a settlement. Employees and immediate family members of Torstar Corp. and D. L. Blair, Inc., their affiliates, subsidiaries and all other agencies, entities and persons connected with the use, marketing or conduct of this contest are not eligible to enter. Taxes on prizes are the sole responsibility of the winner. Acceptance of any prize offered constitutes permission to use winner's name, photograph or other likeness for the purposes of advertising, trade and promotion on behalf of Torstar Corp., its affiliates and subsidiaries without further compensation to the winner, unless prohibited by law.

5. Winner will be determined no later than November 30, 2001, and will be notified by mail. Winner will be required to sign and return an Affidavit of Eligibility/Release of Liability/Publicity Release form within 15 days after winner notification. Noncompliance within that time period may result in disqualification and an alternative winner may be selected. All travelers must execute a Release of Liability prior to ticketing and must possess required travel documents (e.g., passport, photo ID) where applicable. Trip must be booked by December 31, 2001, and completed within one year of notification. No substitution of prize permitted by winner. Torstar Corp. and D. L. Blair, Inc., their parents, affiliates and subsidiaries are not responsible for errors in printing of contest, entries and/or game pieces. In the event of printing or other errors that may result in unintended prize values or duplication of prizes, all affected game pieces or entries shall be null and void. **Purchase or acceptance of a product offer does not improve your chances of winning.**

6. Prizes: (1) Grand Prize—A 2-night/3-day trip for two (2) to New York City, including round-trip coach air transportation nearest winner's home and hotel accommodations (double occupancy) at The Plaza Hotel, a glamorous afternoon makeover at <u>a trendy New York spa,</u> $1,000 in U.S. spending money and an opportunity to <u>have a professional photo taken and appear in a Silhouette advertisement</u> (approximate retail value: $7,000). (10) Ten Runner-Up Prizes of gift packages (retail value $50 ea.). Prizes consist of only those items listed as part of the prize. Limit one prize per person. Prize is valued in U.S. currency.

7. For the name of the winner (available after December 31, 2001) send a self-addressed, stamped envelope to: Harlequin "Silhouette Makes You a Star!" Contest 1197 Winners, P.O. Box 4200 Blair, NE 68009-4200 or you may access the www.eHarlequin.com Web site through February 28, 2002.

Contest sponsored by Torstar Corp., P.O Box 9042, Buffalo, NY 14269-9042.

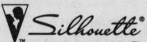

Silhouette® Desire. is proud to present

SONS
OF THE
DESERT

THE SULTANS

**Powerful sheikhs born to rule and destined
to find love as eternal as the sands.**

In three breathtakingly sensual new romances,
Alexandra Sellers continues her bestselling series,
Sons of the Desert. Love and adventure are the destiny
of the three grandsons of the late Sultan of Bagestan,
who must fight to overthrow a ruthless dictator
and restore the sultanate.

Look for these exciting stories:

The Sultan's Heir
(Desire #1379—July 2001)

Undercover Sultan
(Desire #1385—August 2001)

Sleeping with the Sultan
(Desire #1391—September 2001)

Available at your favorite retail outlet.

Silhouette®

Where love comes alive™